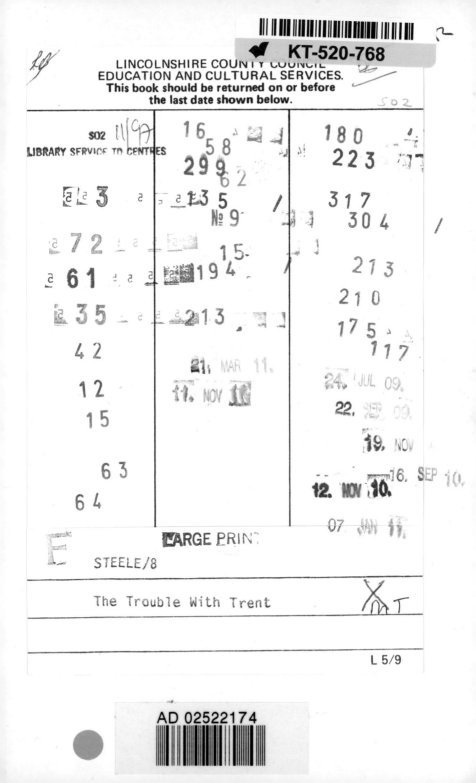

THE TROUBLE WITH TRENT!

THE TROUBLE
WITH TRENT!

BY

JESSICA STEELE

MILLS & BOON®

*MILLS & BOON and
MILLS & BOON with the Rose Device
are registered trademarks of the publisher.*

*First published in Great Britain 1997
Large Print edition 1997
Harlequin Mills & Boon Limited,
Eton House, 18-24 Paradise Road,
Richmond, Surrey TW9 1SR*

© Jessica Steele 1997

ISBN 0 263 15300 2

*Set in Times Roman
16-9710-55550 C16-17¼*

*Printed and bound in Great Britain
by Mackays of Chatham PLC, Chatham*

CHAPTER ONE

ALETHEA was in her bedroom, unsure that she wanted to go to the party. She was not a party animal. A shrill, high-pitched scream rent the air—she changed her mind. Perhaps a party would be preferable to staying home and listening to her niece's temper tantrums. It had all been so peaceful—once!

Up until a month ago life had meandered along at a fairly routine pace. Then, without so much as a warning phone call, her sister Maxine had left her husband.

Alethea had been twelve years old when her sister, her senior by six years, had married Keith Lawrence. 'It won't last!' her mother had proclaimed, not at all in favour of the match. But it had—for ten years.

Then Maxine was back home, and her mother was triumphant. After the children had been tucked up into hurriedly made beds, Maxine had revealed how her husband had confessed that he had been stealing from the firm he worked for.

'I'm not a bit surprised!' her mother had stated bluntly. 'I always knew he was shiftless! That he's a crook as well is all part and parcel of the man!'

At which Maxine had started crying, and then her two-year-old, Polly, who should have been fast asleep, started screaming. Before they knew it, seven-year-old Sadie and five-year-old Georgia were out of bed and coming downstairs, in tears, crying that they wanted to go home.

'Your home is here with Nanna now, darlings.' Their grandmother poured oil on troubled waters, and it took all of an hour to get the children settled again.

'I don't know what I'm going to do,' Maxine fretted when the three of them were in the drawing room again. 'Keith's hoping to pay the money back before the theft is discovered. He's putting the house up for sale and . . .'

'He's selling the house!' Eleanor Pemberton exclaimed. 'He's stolen as much as that?'

'We don't own the house yet. There's a heavy mortgage on it. But there should still be enough in the difference to repay what he took.'

'Why did he take the money in the first place? He knew it wasn't his to take. He was in a trusted position at SEC. He...'

It then transpired that Keith selling their home to discharge his criminal activity was not the sole reason for Maxine leaving him.

'He's having an affair...'

'Typical! And you the mother of his three children!' Mrs Pemberton steamrollered in before Maxine could finish. 'Men!' she scorned—and went off on her favourite theme of males, their fickleness and how there was not one to be trusted.

Alethea's father had left home when she was ten to go and live with someone else. Alethea had grown up having the evils of men being drummed into her daily.

'It's not the first time,' Maxine went on. She had a right, Alethea supposed, to sound as bitter as her mother.

'Are you listening to this, Alethea?' Eleanor Pemberton demanded.

'Every word,' Alethea replied quietly. Her mother's warning about men was there in every look and every sentence. 'Which is why I decided on a career.'

Later that night, the house was, for the moment, silent, and Alethea had space to consider how best she might help her sister. Maxine was a lovely person and it just wasn't right that any man should use her so.

But sympathy on its own would not be much help. It was fortunate that the house had four bedrooms so, with two-year-old Polly sleeping in Maxine's room, and Sadie and Georgia—protesting loudly—sharing another, they were still fairly comfortable.

Alethea was up early the next morning. They lived on the outskirts of London and it was an hour's drive to her office. As usual she took her mother a cup of tea before she left. She contemplated taking Maxine one too. But remembering toddler Polly's screams of the night before—the tot seemed incapable of doing anything at low decibels—she thought that, on balance, Maxine might prefer her not to enter her room and so disturb the sleeping child.

'Is there anything you need?' she had asked her mother.

'I expect Maxine and I will take the girls out for an airing. We'll get anything we need then,' her mother replied. Then her disapproval of men surfaced again. 'I would hope Maxine's learned her lesson after this. My g—'

Alethea could see that her mother was coiling herself up, ready to give forth on the iniquities of the male species. 'I shall have to go—we're very busy at the office just now.'

They had been too. Alethea worked for Gale Drilling International, a huge company. And, at twenty-two, after two years' training and two years as a secretary, she had recently been promoted to Assistant to Hector Chapman's PA, Carol Robinson.

Hector Chapman, for all he was in charge of the whole concern, had a human side to him and was a pleasure to work for. He and Ursula, his wife, were celebrating their silver wedding anniversary in a month's time.

Alethea and Carol, as well as sending out invitations to the dance and buffet, to which they were also invited, were busy in the background dealing with the hotel where the event was to be held, making bookings for long-lost aunts and uncles and dealing with florists. In addition to their other work, they were making sure that nothing could go wrong.

Alethea went home after another exhausting but stimulating day to find that the house, which last night she had considered 'fairly comfortable' for the six of them, had undergone something of a change. Maxine's furniture had arrived.

'You don't mind, do you?' Maxine asked anxiously as she followed Alethea into her bedroom.

Alethea stared at her once roomy bedroom, which now housed an extra wardrobe, a couple of easy chairs and a sofa. Sympathy, she recalled thinking less than twenty-four hours ago, would not be of much help.

'Of course I don't,' she answered stoutly. 'I'm—er—just a bit surprised. I had an idea furniture removers took an age to organise.'

'You know Mother. She hired a van, and got the chap who comes to do the garden to bring his pal and do some heavy carrying. Sadie droned on endlessly at breakfast about having to share a bed with Georgia, so Mother said it was common sense to go and fetch their two beds and anything else I might need, before Keith sold the furniture as well as the house.'

'I didn't see why he should let his *other woman* have any of the stuff that Maxine's cared for all these years.' Eleanor Pemberton joined them in the bedroom.

Alethea could just see it: no doubt her mother had gone to Maxine's house, taken a look around—and taken charge!

A month later, they could barely move for furniture. Because in their own adequately furnished house they now had what Alethea was sure must be the entire contents of Maxine's home. Barking one's shins against something or other became an everyday hazard.

And still Polly's screaming went on. There was nothing wrong with the child apparently, except temper—she had the lungs of an opera singer in her prime.

Time to party! Alethea stared at her reflection in the full-length mirror. Honest violet eyes stared back at her. She skimmed her glance over her blonde hair, which fell straight to her chin and then just turned under.

Was her dress too short? She had few party clothes and had bought this dress specifically for Mr and Mrs Chapman's anniversary party. It was a violet-blue that matched her eyes. She had good legs, long legs—but the dress had not seemed so short in the shop. Only now, in the privacy of her room, did it seem a shade on the skimpy side. Perfectly plain, with narrow shoulder straps, it was cut to flare gently from the hips.

She was just assuring herself that perhaps she had made a good choice after all when her bedroom door opened. Privacy? It was a thing of the past. Her seven-year-old niece came in.

'Sorry,' Sadie apologised. She was rather a nice child when she wasn't complaining. 'I didn't know you were changing.'

'I'm changed.' Alethea smiled.

'You're going to your party in your petticoat?'

Oh, grief! Alethea was just about to die when her sister came in. 'Out!' Maxine instructed her daughter.

'Sadie thinks this dress looks like a petticoat,' Alethea panicked.

'Rot! You'll see shorter skirts there,' Maxine told her bracingly.

To Alethea's relief, Maxine was proved right. In fact, given that the hem was inches above her knees, her dress looked positively decorous beside the thigh-length outfits that some were wearing.

Alethea had called for Carol Robinson on her way, and both Mr and Mrs Chapman had greeted them warmly when they arrived at the hotel. 'You're not on duty tonight—you're here to enjoy yourself,' Hector Chapman had reminded them.

It was fun chatting to all and sundry, Alethea discovered. Fun being able to put faces to names on the invitation list Mrs Chapman had given her. Fun to dance without the remotest inclination to be more involved.

Carol Robinson was fun too. Alethea knew Carol was thirty-three and dedicated to her work but was amazed when, during a medley of dances that went back to before the flood, someone asked Carol to Charleston with him—and she agreed.

My giddy aunt! Alethea's lovely violet eyes widened. Never had she suspected Carol of such expertise! She was so superbly efficient in the office, Alethea had never guessed her capable of letting her hair down to this degree.

Unbeknown to her, Alethea wore a gentle smile as she glanced away from the dancers. She looked up to her right—and her breath caught. There, about ten yards away, was one person, she discovered, who was not watching the dancing. He was tall, dark-haired, somewhere in his mid-thirties, and was staring at her!

Hurriedly Alethea looked back to where Carol was still showing no sign of flagging. But this time Carol's flashing feet had less of an impact on Alethea. Who was he? Why was he watching her and not the dancers? And for how long *had* he been watching her?

Somehow, for all that she had not exchanged so much as a single word with the man, Alethea felt shaken by having met him. Rot, she admonished herself, not ready to believe it. Yet...

Just then the music ended and a breathless Carol headed her way. 'Whew! I'm hot. I'm going for a drink. Can I get you something?' she offered.

Alethea declined and, as if by some magnetic pull, felt an almost overwhelming compulsion to look to her right to see if the tall, dark-haired man was still there. It took a very determined effort not to.

She gave her attention to the MC, who was announcing that the next dance in the selection would be a Viennese waltz. Alethea then discovered that the man who, a few minutes earlier, had been watching her was standing right in front of her.

She was tall but she still had to look up. Her honest violet eyes met his dark ones, and her heart, for some reason, did a little somersault.

'Are you going to dance with me?' he asked. He had a warm, rather pleasant kind of voice.

'I don't...' she began.

'You don't know me.' With a hint of a smile he finished what she had *not* been going to say! Clearly he was a man who had no time for obstacles in his way, for he straightway rectified that omission. 'Trent de Havilland,' he introduced himself.

De Havilland rang a bell. She'd typed it on one of the invitation envelopes. 'How do you do?' she found herself murmuring.

'And you are?'

Alethea had been brought up to be wary of men, but they were in a crowded room, for goodness' sake. And while Trent de Havilland was sophisticated to the nth degree, he was hardly likely to carry her off to his evil lair in front of everyone.

'Alethea Pemberton,' she answered quickly, starting to feel she was no end of a fool for delaying so long.

That hint of a smile on his well-formed mouth grew. 'And where do you come from, Alethea Pemberton?' he wanted to know.

Alethea was backed up against a brick wall of caution. But she felt it was fairly safe to reveal, 'I work in Mr Chapman's office.'

'There, now we know all about each other,' he commented, when in fact all she knew about him was his name. 'Let's dance.'

'I don't dance.' She stopped him quickly before he could guide her to the dance area.

'How could you lie to me?' he reproached teasingly, not moving, just standing there looking down at her.

'I'm sorry,' she apologised at once, realising he might have caught a glimpse of her dancing already. 'What I meant to say...' she went on. At work she was unflappable, at home she was unflappable, so why, all of a sudden, standing here with this man, was she getting all confused? 'What I meant to say was, that I don't Viennese waltz. I can't.'

Trent de Havilland leaned back. 'Can you count to six?' he enquired. It seemed her apology was accepted, because, without waiting for her to reply, he caught her elbow in a firm hold and took her to the dance area.

Nervousness made Alethea fumble over the first few steps but, after less than ten seconds' tuition, she was floating. Trent de Havilland was holding her firmly, neither too close nor too far away, his right hand steady at her back, his left hand clasping her right as he guided her elegantly over the floor.

Round and around they went, in perfect rhythm with the music. There was something magical about it. Alethea felt as if she were in another era, dressed not in some violet slip of a dress, but in some magnificent ball gown and bejewelled.

What Trent de Havilland was thinking or feeling she had not the smallest clue, because while other couples circling the floor were in occasional conversation, he didn't say a word.

Someone almost cannoned into them. Trent pulled her closer. She caught her breath again, indeed, felt the oddest difficulty in breathing at all as he held her against him for long seconds after he had drawn her out of harm's way.

She looked up into his dark eyes. It was as if no one else existed, as if it were just the two of them. His eyes, those warm, dark eyes, seemed to search down into her very soul.

Some small sound escaped her—she didn't know what to say. Her lips parted and he transferred his gaze down from her eyes. She felt his hand on her back pulling her close to him, and her whole body tingled.

Then the music stopped. Alethea had been aware of it, but abruptly snapped out of her trance-like state.

She realised too that her partner was no longer holding her. He had taken a step away. She searched for something to say—a murmured 'thank you' would have done. But she felt too tongue-tied to say anything. A moment later she discovered that comments from her were not required. Because, without saying one word himself, Trent de Havilland once more touched a hand to her elbow and escorted her off the floor. And—still silent—went striding from her view.

'I didn't know you could Viennese waltz!' Carol exclaimed, appearing from nowhere, while Alethea was still striving to come back to earth.

'Your Charleston beat everything into a cocked hat!' Alethea somehow found the wit to respond.

Alethea did not see Trent de Havilland again that evening. Not that she consciously looked for him—it was just that he wasn't around. Perhaps he'd just looked in out of courtesy, stayed for one dance, and then legged it out of there to follow his more normal Saturday night pursuits. Not that she was in the least interested, anyhow!

At midnight Carol asked her how she felt about leaving. 'Fine by me,' Alethea replied, and, after exchanging a few pleasantries with their hosts, they said their goodbyes. Alethea dropped Carol off on the way to her own home.

'Nice party?' Maxine enquired the next morning.

Thinking about it, Alethea realised that, yes, it had been. 'Very nice,' she replied.

'Anyone special there?' Maxine wanted to know.

Why Alethea should have a sudden picture in her mind's eye of tall, dark, sophisticated Trent de Havilland, she couldn't have said. But she did not have time to wonder for long, because her mother, acid in every syllable, butted in to chide, 'If by "special" you mean some man, then I hope to Heaven that Alethea has more sense!'

'There wasn't anyone special there,' Alethea denied mildly. But, ridiculously, she found she wanted to smile as a voice in her ear reproached, How could you lie...?

The rest of the day passed off noisily—with only a short period of quiet when, exhausted, Polly had a nap. Alethea's two older nieces were quite interesting when they weren't squabbling. But she was glad to see Monday. Somehow, for all that life in the office was most often hectic, it seemed more tranquil than home.

She drove to work musing, at first not very seriously, that perhaps she should consider moving out. Maybe find a flat somewhere. Then, staying with the notion, she realised that there seemed to be a lot going for it.

Maxine had seen neither hide nor hair of her husband since she had left him. They were in telephone communication; she knew that. Maxine shed floods of tears when she rang Keith, often about the non-appearance of the maintenance money he kept promising but which never materialised.

But it was all of a month now since Maxine had left him and had she had any thoughts of going back to him, then Alethea felt she would have seen some sign of them by now.

Life at home went from her mind the moment she arrived at the office she shared with Carol. There was the usual buzz about the place and, as ever, they were busy.

Carol was closeted with Mr Chapman around mid-afternoon when Alethea looked at the 'Celebrations' file she had opened to check what accounts might be outstanding. She came across the guest list.

Without fully realising what she was doing, she skimmed her gaze over the names. She halted at de Havilland. Halted, and paused for some moments, for while almost every other invitation had been sent to couples, the invitation to the man who had so elegantly waltzed her around the dance floor had been sent to Trent alone. 'Mr Trenton de Havilland,' she read—and was back in his arms, back on the dance floor, the music was playing, the . . .

'Have you time to do this for me?' Carol who clearly had more than enough to do, if the paperwork in her hands was anything to go by, brought Alethea quickly back to earth.

'Of course,' she smiled obligingly, and went home that evening a little later than normal but satisfied with her day.

She let herself in; the house was noisy. It seemed that the children were as boundlessly energetic and as vocal as ever. She earned herself another bruise as she knocked into a chest of drawers that stood in the hall simply because there was no other place to put it— and found she was again thinking, a little more seriously this time, that perhaps it might not be such a bad idea after all to find somewhere else to live.

Despite Polly being such a bad-tempered child, there was something quite loveable about her. She had such a beam of a smile that it had them all forgiving her every misdeed. But there was no sign of that smile about her later in the evening when, around eight-thirty, she was brought downstairs so as not to disturb Sadie and Georgia who were already asleep. Polly had decided that *she* wasn't going to go to sleep. She yelled and screamed, and held her breath, and quite terrified Alethea lest she never breathed again. So that when, at last, she finally exhausted herself and did fall asleep, the adults were feeling very much frazzled.

'You must be hating like crazy the fact that we moved in and shattered the peace and calm of your life,' Maxine opined as she flopped in a chair and gratefully accepted the cup of coffee Alethea handed her.

'Nonsense!' her mother decried stoutly. Alethea knew she never had wanted Maxine to leave home in the first place and was delighted to have her back again. Her mother was impervious, it seemed, to the chaos about her.

The phone rang and Maxine went to get up. 'I'll get it,' Alethea volunteered, instructing herself to be polite if it was her uncaring brother-in-law calling to tell his wife why he wasn't able to pay her any maintenance this week either.

But the call wasn't for Maxine, nor was it for her mother. 'Hello,' Alethea said, into the receiver.

She went hot all over when, after a moment's pause, a firm voice answered pleasantly, 'Hello, Alethea, Trent de Havilland.'

She'd known that—even though she could not believe it. She had just *known* that it was his voice. 'Oh, hello,' she said lightly, and, feeling confused and jumbled up again and totally unlike her real self, asked, 'What can I do for you?'

Perhaps he needed Mr Chapman's home number to ring and thank him for Saturday, or something of that sort.

That, it transpired, was not the reason for Trent's call. Her unflappable self disappeared when he came straight to the point of his call: 'I'd like you to have dinner with me tomorrow. Are you free?' he asked.

Alethea opened her mouth. 'I . . .' she began. Half of her head still believed this was a business call and she almost asked, In what connection? Rapidly she got herself together. Only he jumped in before she could formulate the words she wanted—in truth she didn't know what they were!

'Good,' Trent stated, and, continuing every bit as if she had just accepted his invitation, he said, 'I'll call for you at seven.'

Alethea came rapidly out of the confusion his call had instigated. 'Presumably you know where I live?' she questioned faintly.

'Goodnight,' he said, and the phone went dead.

Alethea stared at the receiver in her hand with astonishment. Had she just agreed to go out with the man who, it had to be admitted, seemed to have a knack of disturbing her previously unflappable self?

Apparently she had. Though, from what she could remember, he had given her very little chance to refuse.

CHAPTER TWO

BY MORNING Alethea had decided that she would ring Trent de Havilland and tell him that she was not going to go to dinner with him. She would tell him that she had been so surprised by his call, she hadn't had a chance to recall a prior engagement. Into her mind loomed the thought of another evening of Polly deciding she did not want to go to sleep and, what was more, she was *never* going to sleep—and if she wasn't ever going to go to sleep, the whole world was going to hear about it.

Hating herself for thinking that it would be quite nice to have a tantrum-free evening, Alethea took her mother a cup of tea and went to her office, where she found time during the day only to discover that Trenton de Havilland's home phone number wasn't listed. With Mr Chapman dashing to various meetings, she had no chance to ask him if he had Trent's number. Or, failing that, if Mr

26

Chapman knew where Trenton de Havilland worked.

'Bye, Alethea,' Carol said when they parted in the car park twenty minutes after five.

'Bye,' Alethea smiled, and drove home with her tummy all of a flutter. She had been out on dates before, but only with men she had known for some while—and never with any man like Trent!

'Dinner will be late,' her mother greeted her. 'We've had such a day of it.'

'Polly playing up?' Alethea guessed.

'She's been as good as gold.' Her mother purred as if the high voltage tot had never ever known a temper tantrum. 'We went to the house—it hasn't been sold yet—and *he* was there.'

'Keith?'

'Who else? He's been suspended.'

'SEC have found out about the missing money?'

Her mother nodded. 'They're investigating. I couldn't resist telling him a few home truths. He called me an interfering old bat! Can you imagine?'

There was more in the same vein. Eleanor Pemberton only broke off momentarily when

Maxine came into the room, looking as if she'd been crying. Alethea guessed that her sister had heard more than enough of what her mother had to say on the subject of her husband, and broke in quickly, 'Actually, I'm going out to dinner this evening, so I won't be needing—'

'With Carol?' her mother asked sharply, her thoughts swiftly taken away from the man her other daughter had married.

'No—er—a—an acquaintance.'

'A male acquaintance?' her mother fired at her before she could add more. 'You never did get round to saying who phoned last night—is it him?'

'Yes, actually.'

'Hrmph,' her mother grunted. 'Do I know him?' was the next question. Alethea had been through the third degree on several occasions before.

'I'll introduce you; he's calling for me at seven,' she replied, and quickly made her escape to go and shower and change, and to wonder why if, as she told herself, she did not want to go out with Mr Trenton de Havilland, she should feel so churned up; somehow she was very wary, yet at the same time she was experiencing a prickle of excitement at the prospect.

Alethea found it a rush to be ready on time. Sadie and Georgia came in to help—which added another five minutes.

A high-pitched squabble broke out between the two little girls when they both wanted to use her face powder at the same time. However, having separated them and placated them with a spray of perfume behind their ears, Alethea and her two 'helpers' finally left her room with one minute to go before seven.

She knew that, good manners aside, there was no way in which she was going to be able to avoid introducing her escort to her family, but she was hopeful of making that introduction as brief as possible.

It was not that she was ashamed of her family in any way. It was just that Trenton de Havilland was a very sophisticated man. She wanted him out of there before her mother attempted to give him the grilling which had been the fate of her other escorts.

'Aunt Alethea gave us a squirt with her perfume...' The girls rushed ahead of her into the sitting room—and stopped dead.

A prickle of apprehension had already started along Alethea's spine as she followed them. She, too, stopped dead. Trent de Havilland had already arrived! The strained atmosphere spoke volumes.

How long he had been closeted with her mother and her sister and, for once, an angelic-looking Polly, Alethea had no idea. She hadn't heard his car, though perhaps with Sadie and Georgia squawking in her bedroom that wasn't so surprising.

'I'm sorry I wasn't here to introduce you.' She smiled as she went into the room, trying to ignore the fact that her mother looked as if she'd been on a diet of vinegar for a week. Maxine was looking much the same—what on earth had been going on?

'I was several minutes early.' Trent had risen to his feet as, in a mustard-shade dress, she'd entered the room. He paused to say hello to Sadie and Georgia, and started to come over to her. 'I introduced myself,' he commented easily. But, for all his relaxed manner, he seemed not inclined to delay their departure. 'Shall we go?'

They said their goodbyes, and Alethea led the way out into the hall, followed by her mother's sharp warning, 'Don't forget you have to be up early for work in the morning, Alethea!'

Oh, grief! She skirted the chest of drawers and heard a thudding sound as Trent didn't, and just knew that the evening was going to be a disaster before it began.

'I'm sorry about that,' she apologised tensely, already guessing that her mother had asked him some pretty pertinent questions and he was probably ready to call the evening off right then and there.

'Sorry?' he queried, opening the passenger door of a black, extremely expensive car that suggested that whatever job he did, he was well paid for it.

Loyalty to her family, plus a sudden realisation that, whatever had passed between him, her mother and sister—Maxine had been looking on the sour side too—she did not want to know about it, made her say, 'At a guess, I'd say you cracked your shin on that chest in the hall.'

'Is it there as some sort of test you give to all your men friends—to see how brave they are?'

'You didn't cry,' she replied—and suddenly the tension was eased, and they were both laughing.

Miraculously, though she rather knew Trent had a lot to do with it, the evening which she thought had started off badly progressed to a fine start.

He took her to a restaurant which served excellent food. But she had little recollection of what she ate, for he was an excellent dinner companion: witty, serious, knowledgable.

'Yes, but, Trent—er—Trenton...' She went on to put forward her point of view, but the subject went straight from her mind. It was the confusion he seemed to have a knack of arousing in her. She started to grow hot at the thought that this astute man who had introduced himself to her as Trent de Havilland might think she had been checking up on him, and had found out his name was Trenton. 'It's on file—your name.' She dug a bigger hole for herself. Oh, Heavens, this was dreadful. 'I wasn't checking up on you!' she blurted out.

'That's not very flattering of you,' he teased.

She started to feel a bit better. Enough, anyway, to be able to explain, 'I was checking Mr Chapman's silver wedding celebrations file, ready to finalise everything before putting it to bed. Your name was on the guest list.'

Trent smiled and, as if realising from the gentle tide of pink that had washed her skin that she had been feeling a trifle awkward, he smoothly turned the conversation to enquire, 'You enjoy working for Hector?'

'Very much,' she answered, but felt honour bound to add, 'Though I'm not his PA. She's Carol Robinson and I assist her.' Alethea's voice started to fade as it suddenly dawned on her that he probably knew that anyway. 'Didn't Mr Chapman want to know what you wanted my address and phone number for?' she asked, and had to admit that she liked the way Trent de Havilland's mouth quirked at the corners whenever she managed to amuse him.

'You're too sharp to be a mere assistant,' he responded charmingly.

She enjoyed his charm, though she had sense enough to see that it wouldn't take a genius to guess from where he had obtained the information he needed. Though Hector

Chapman giving that information spoke volumes. She knew, indisputably, that Mr Chapman would never have imparted anything about her unless the enquirer was not only very well known to him, but also a man whom he knew to be trustworthy.

Given that she had been brought up to be distrustful of all men, Alethea was feeling more relaxed with Trent than with any man she'd ever known. To suddenly realise, too, that she already had all the evidence she needed, because Trent must be well known to her boss to have been invited to his anniversary celebration, only went to make her feel even more relaxed.

Relaxed, and able to ask him what she considered to be a most natural question, 'What sort of work do *you* do?'

'I'm in science engineering,' he answered.

'Well, that leaves me dead in the water,' Alethea laughed, 'Science was my worst subject at school.'

'I'm sure you were brilliant at others,' he commented. 'So tell me more about you.'

For no reason, she started to feel tense again. 'There's nothing to tell,' she replied.

He wasn't having that. 'You live at home with your mother and sister—plus your sister's children,' he documented. How much had he guessed? Alethea started to feel wary of him. 'Are there no men in your household?' he asked, and Alethea, knowing she was being prickly, but somehow unable to help it, resented his questioning.

'Are there any women in yours?' she asked bluntly.

'I live alone,' he answered quite openly, adding drily, 'though it's true that I have a dear soul who comes in and sets the place to order three times a week.'

There were traces of a smile about his expression, but suddenly the evening was going badly for Alethea and she could not respond. 'Have you ever been married?' she asked abruptly.

Trent he Havilland studied her unsmiling face for some seconds, as if trying to gauge what, if anything, lay behind her question. 'No, never,' he stated at last. But his eyes were alert, his expression all at once unsmiling. 'Have you?'

'Good Heavens, no!' Alethea exclaimed.

'You sound as if you find the idea appalling?' he suggested, his dark eyes steady on her violet ones.

Suddenly her tension vanished, and her sense of humour quite unexpectedly bubbled to the surface. 'So long as you weren't asking,' she replied and, when his eyes remained unflinching on hers, she continued, 'I should hate to hurt your feelings.'

'Like hell you would,' he rejoined.

'I'd never hurt anyone on purpose,' she informed him coolly.

Her coolness didn't so much as touch him. 'Turn them down gently—is that your motto?' he surmised, as if he truly thought she must have received several marriage proposals by now. She wasn't interested in marriage, for goodness' sake! Nor did she care much for the subject under discussion, she decided. Though, before she could open her mouth to change it, she discovered that Trent had had enough of it too, and was heading in another direction himself to ask, 'May I enquire after your father?'

Alethea was not sure that she cared for this new subject any better. 'My father?' she prevaricated.

'He doesn't live at home?' Trent pursued, not a man to give up easily, even if her look did have a chilly edge to it.

Had her mother told him that? She did not want to think so. But, much as she loved her parent, she was not blind to the fact that her mother could be manipulative when it suited her. She remembered the sour expressions on both her mother's and her sister's faces when she had gone into the sitting room. And, even though she had earlier been convinced that she didn't want to know what had gone on in that room before she had come downstairs, she found she was asking in a rush, 'What did my mother say to you?'

'Nothing to cause such distress in those beautiful violet eyes,' he answered. Quite gently, she thought, but it was a non-answer just the same.

'So tell me,' she insisted.

He shrugged, but he was watchful as he revealed, 'Apparently you're more interested in your career than you are in men.'

She could cope with that. 'Anything wrong in that?' she asked.

'Not a thing,' he replied pleasantly. Only, remembering her mother's expression, Alethea couldn't leave it there.

'And?' she further insisted.

'You're a devil for punishment,' he murmured lightly.

'So?'

'At the risk of sounding ungallant, I don't believe it.'

'This is like drawing teeth!' she exclaimed frustratedly. 'Don't believe what?'

'You have beautiful teeth too,' he said, delaying a moment more. But, having flattered her, he went on to reveal the appalling truth. 'According to your mother—though I must say she couched it in much better terms... basically what she meant to convey was that you are only going out with me in the interests of career advancement.'

Alethea, innocent of all charges, went scarlet. 'I... You...' she tried, but was rendered temporarily speechless. It was left to Trent, his eyes on her unhappy colour, to try to make her feel better.

'I'm too conceited to believe that, of course.' He attempted to coax a smile out of her.

Alethea could not have smiled had her life depended upon it. How could her mother have said such a thing? She would have liked to have believed otherwise, of course, but she knew her mother. 'You have your own company, don't you?' she guessed.

'I do,' he owned.

'You told my mother, and...'

'I didn't so much as tell her—just gave her my name.'

Her mother never ceased to amaze her. Some days she never went outside the house and yet, when Alethea arrived home from work, her mother was up to date on all the gossip. But now, local gossip aside, it seemed her mother had mental index cards on the London business world!

'Shall we go?' she offered bluntly. The coffee they had ordered to finish their meal had only just arrived, but her sensitivity was such that she was wondering why Trent hadn't left her home there and then, without waiting for her to present herself downstairs. That was what her mother had wanted, of course.

'You're not going to let what I've told you spoil what has been a very pleasurable evening for me—and I hope for you too—are you?'

'Trent—I . . .' Alethea halted, and realised that, in addition to her mother not wanting her evening with Trent to start, her parent would be quite pleased, if, since start it had, it should end badly. Alethea knew her mother hadn't wanted Maxine to leave home and thereby break her mother's sphere of influence. Mother had done everything in her power to prevent Maxine's marriage. But, from what Alethea could see now, her mother wasn't waiting for her to go so far as to become involved with anyone. At the first sign that Alethea was going out with any man who might be strong-minded, her mother was out to nip in the bud any remote possibility that might lead to her other daughter leaving home. Alethea took a shaky breath, and stared across into a pair of dark eyes that were silently, steadily watching her. 'To answer your question,' she said, 'my father left home when I was ten.'

Trent's look was warm and encouraging. 'For another woman,' he stated, seeming to know it for a fact, though Alethea hardly thought that her mother had imparted that piece of knowledge.

Normally Alethea would have clammed up on the subject, but just then she was feeling cross enough with her mother not to care. Alethea knew full well that, should she challenge her mother tomorrow over what she had told Trent, Mrs Pemberton would tell her she was making a fuss over nothing.

'Yes, for another woman,' she confirmed, whether Trent needed confirmation or not.

'And your mother thereafter set about trying to see to it that no man came near you or your sister.' He paused a moment, then commented lightly, 'Um—she seems to have failed miserably with your sister—I counted three children.'

'She has only three,' Alethea stated, Trent's manner and his humour causing her to feel better.

'But their father, or fathers, aren't allowed inside the house?' he suggested.

Alethea shook her head. 'Maxine married. Only her marriage recently broke up.'

'That's a pity,' he commented, and Alethea was unsure if he meant for the children's sake, Maxine's sake, or marriage's sake. 'It can't be easy for her,' he added.

'Apparently it wasn't the first time her husband's eye had wandered,' Alethea said, not wanting Trent to think that her dear sister was in any way to blame for the marriage split.

'But this time she decided to return home?'

'Bringing her furniture with her,' Alethea commented, not wanting to tell him the other, more dishonest facts of it, and wondering if Trent would be nursing a bruise on his shin tomorrow.

'So that accounts for the chest in the hall,' he grinned.

'We are a touch overcrowded,' she laughed, and was suddenly feeling good again. She heard herself tack on, 'I've been toying with the idea of moving out and finding a place of my own—though I don't suppose I will.'

'Your mother wouldn't let you?'

Honestly! Instantly she was up in arms. 'I'm twenty-two!' she informed Trent crossly. 'The decision is mine.' She stared with hostility at him, sparks of annoyance flaring in her eyes. But, as she looked at his dark, unwavering gaze, so she glimpsed a dancing light. He, she realised, had aggravated her deliberately! 'Provoking devil!' she mumbled, but had to smile. 'I think it's time I went home,' she stated.

Trent settled the bill and, without comment, escorted her outside. Though just when she was starting to think, in a slightly miffed way, that he'd had enough and couldn't wait to drop her off at her door, he sent that notion clear out of her head by offering, 'With your house so overcrowded, shall we go back to mine for coffee?'

'I've just had coffee,' she reminded him, feeling better that he seemed to want to prolong the evening. But he was the sophisticated type and she was not green; coffee could well be another word for what he was actually offering!

'I thought we might talk, get to know each other,' he answered, as he saw her into his car.

I'll bet! Alethea waited until he joined her in the car. 'We've been talking all night,' she thought to mention.

'All I've learned about you, apart from my observations on your sensitivity and sincerity, is that you live in an overcrowded household of women, that you may or may not be intending to find somewhere less overcrowded, and might I suggest—if the high-pitched squealing that was going on when I arrived is anything to go by—you need somewhere a little more peaceful to live. I've also discovered that you work as an assistant PA.'

'That isn't enough?'

Her words had sounded sharp, she realised, when Trent looked at her long and hard. But whatever he was thinking, his manner remained mild. 'Should we row on our first date?' he asked.

First date! She liked him; she must do, or she would not be here now. But at his hint of a second date she felt wary. 'I'll take you to your home,' he said before she could make up her mind how she felt about going out with him again.

Trent drove easily, effortlessly, and in no time at all it seemed that they were pulling up outside her home. When he got out of the car and came round to her door, Alethea got out feeling nervous and unsure.

She wouldn't ask him in. Lord knew what surprises awaited them—her embittered mother had had hours in which to build up a fine head of vitriol. Or perhaps Maxine was walking the downstairs rooms trying to pacify a wailing Polly.

At the door she turned. 'Thank you for a pleasant evening,' she trotted out, and was all jittery inside. Silently, unspeaking, he stared down at her in the porch light. She didn't know if he would try to kiss her, nor how she would react if he did. As yet she had formulated no answer, should he ask for the second date he had hinted at.

But Alethea was totally mystified when Trent neither attempted to kiss her nor to ask her out again. But, his tone even—he could have been discussing the weather—he replied civilly, 'The pleasure was mine. Goodnight, Alethea.' And with that he went back to his car.

Alethea did not want to see him drive off. Motivated by pride that insisted he should not go away with any idiotic notion that she might be hanging on his every word and deed, she did a rapid about-turn and swiftly let herself in through the front door.

Only when she had the door shut—she was on the inside and he was on the outside—did she pause to take stock. He hadn't so much as *tried* to kiss her, much less ask her out again! Not that she'd have gone out with him again if he had asked, she firmly decided. But then all thoughts of Trent de Havilland were momentarily taken from her mind when the stair light came on and her sister came hurrying into view.

'Has he gone?' Maxine whispered, leaning over the bannister rail, either because of the possibility of Trent de Havilland still being around, or because she was scared of waking one of the children.

'Yes, just,' Alethea whispered back.

'Shall I make you some hot chocolate?'

By the sound of it, Maxine wanted to talk. 'Lovely,' Alethea accepted, and the two of them went quietly into the kitchen.

It was there that Alethea soon realised that her sister's need to talk did not stem from a loneliness of spirit, as she had supposed, but from an urgent need to have a discussion that would not wait until morning, when there was every chance they would be interrupted.

For, without so much as enquiring, Did you have a nice evening?, Maxine launched in to ask, 'Do you know who Trenton de Havilland is?'

Alethea stared at her. Trent had introduced himself to Maxine and their mother as Trenton? But she concentrated on Maxine's question. Alethea knew that Trent was a nifty Viennese waltzer, was interesting, not to say stimulating to go out with, and also that he was a friend of her employer. But Maxine had asked if she knew who he was. 'Who is he?' Alethea queried.

'He didn't tell you that he owns Science Engineering and Consulting?' Maxine pressed.

'I know he has his own company,' Alethea answered, feeling slightly perplexed and wanting to know what Maxine was getting into a state about, for she was certainly growing more and more agitated by the second. 'He told me he was in science engineering, but...' Alethea broke off suddenly, remembering how Trent had only had to mention his name for it to mean something to her mother. 'Are you saying that, like Mother, you know of his business?'

'I should do—Keith works for him!'

'Keith...' Alethea stopped, horrified, Science Engineering and Consulting suddenly clicking in her head to be SEC, who had suspended her brother-in-law while investigations into his honesty were taking place! Oh, my stars, her brother-in-law was employed in a trusted position by Trent and had abused that trust. 'Does Trent know Keith works for him?' she asked, alarmed.

'Heavens, no. Keith's not that far up the corporate tree that his chairman would know of his existence!'

That was some small relief to Alethea. She felt she would never have survived the embarrassment had Trent known all the time he had sat opposite her this evening that her brother-in-law, his employee, was a crook who had robbed him. 'Mother knew all about Trent being the man who pays Keith's salary, though, didn't she?'

'She saw Keith's letter today from SEC. It had the name of the chairman and directors on it. You know Mother's sharp brain. She'll have filed away all that information without even realising she was doing it.'

'Oh, grief!' Alethea exclaimed, and remembered how both her mother and sister had looked when she had come into the sitting room at a minute before seven that evening. 'Mother seems to be permanently bitter about men. But is that why *you* looked a degree or two more sour when Trent was here? Because...'

'How else could I look?' Maxine asked tearfully. 'Here am I stuck in this house which, since Mother insisted I bring everything that wasn't nailed down so that some other woman couldn't have it, is so crammed full you can't move without tripping over, and there were you, all dressed up to go out for a fun evening with a man who I'd just realised could be ultimately responsible for bringing a court action against my children's father!'

'Oh, Maxine!' Alethea exclaimed as her sister started to cry. Men, men, rotten men, she fumed as she hurried over to her.

Alethea wasn't sure that she meant all men as she tried to comfort her sister. When Maxine was a little calmer, she made her the drink which Maxine had offered to make her. And when, half an hour later, she and her sister were upstairs and in their rooms, one thing was set like concrete in Alethea's mind. Maxine's disclosures about who was in charge of SEC made it well and truly settled. Even if Trent de Havilland did make contact to ask her for a second date, now that she knew that, ultimately, he was the man her brother-in-law had stolen from, there was no way she could ever go out with him again!

CHAPTER THREE

WEDNESDAY and Thursday passed uneventfully, although Alethea found that thoughts of Trent de Havilland were slipping into her head far more frequently than she would have expected—given that she was never going to go out with him again, even if he did ask...which he wouldn't.

Evidence that Trent de Havilland was not thinking of her so frequently—if at all—was plain from the fact that her phone at home stayed silent. Not that she was at all bothered, of course. It saved her from looking for some excuse to give him. How could she go out with him when her sister's husband had cheated his firm out of money?

Life at home, however, seemed to be growing increasingly difficult. Her mother was forever badgering her on the subject of Trent de Havilland, even though Alethea had stated that she had no intention of going out with him again. No need to tell her mother that chance would be a fine thing—a girl had her pride.

'The children have been up in your room,' her mother greeted her when she arrived home from work on Friday.

'All of them?' Alethea asked faintly.

'Just Sadie and Georgia. I looked after them after school while Maxine took Polly to the doctor. I don't think they did any harm.'

'How is Polly?'

'It's just a bit of a cold. The doctor said there's nothing to worry about.'

Bracing herself, Alethea went upstairs to her room. 'Oh, grief!' she muttered as she went in. Someone had added an extra table to the room, which was already filled to capacity, and her wardrobe door was ajar. Her clothes had been gone through, garments tried on and then crumpled by the inexpert attempts of shorter persons to hang them back on the rail. Her dressing table was a disaster area. The idea of having an apartment of her own had more and more appeal. Her mother would have a fit if she suggested leaving home, she knew that in advance, but...

Sadie and Georgia, of course, had no school the following day and were allowed to stay up a little later—if they were quiet. But they seemed to be noisier than ever that evening. Alethea joined in the general sigh of relief when at last all three girls were in bed and silence reigned.

Then the telephone rang. Most peculiarly, for there was not the smallest reason why, Alethea felt her heartbeat quicken. She looked across at Maxine. 'It's for you, I expect,' she commented, but Maxine was already halfway out of her chair.

'She's far too soft with him!' Eleanor Pemberton stated abruptly as Maxine disappeared into the hall to take the call in the alcove under the stairs. 'What she wants to do is—' She broke off as Maxine came back into the room.

'It's for you, Alethea,' Maxine informed her.

'Who is it?' their mother wanted to know.

'Trent de Havilland,' Maxine answered, and Alethea felt her face go a warm pink.

'I thought you weren't going to go out with him again!' Eleanor Pemberton snapped.

'I'm not,' Alethea answered, and went out into the hall. Why on earth she felt the need to swallow before she could pick up the phone and say, 'Hello,' she had no idea.

'Lucky I caught you in!' Trent responded. Was he being funny?

'You're on your way out yourself, I expect,' she commented lightly, hoping he'd think that was the way it was with her, too, and that the sun never set for her on a Friday night.

'I'm just back after a few days in Italy,' he drawled easily, and, getting down to the point of his call, he continued, 'I'm having some people round tomorrow evening—any time from eight to midnight. Can you make it?'

He did want to see her again! She wasn't going, of course, but, she realised, she felt much better for being asked. 'I'm sorry,' she began, useless when it came to telling lies, but striving hard to think up some excuse.

'It was a long shot,' he cut in pleasantly. 'I hardly expected you'd be free.'

'You know how it is,' she murmured, wondering why she didn't tell him outright that she was not going to see him again—probably because she was certain to receive a very short and sharp answer for her trouble. Or perhaps it was solely good manners that held her back.

'Of course,' he answered blandly, but straight away he went on to astonish her by adding, 'Perhaps you'll make a note of my address. If you and your date are in the area, both of you might like to drop in.'

She hadn't found his address on file at the office. So, like the efficient assistant PA that she was, Alethea automatically had a notepad before her, a pencil in her hand, as Trent dictated his address. Don't hold your breath, she thought sourly—clearly Trent de Havilland didn't give a button that she had a date with someone else tomorrow—and he wasn't to know that she hadn't, was he! Not that she wanted him to give a button anyway! 'I'll see what I can do—thank you for asking,' she said prettily, and knew, as she was sure Trent knew, that his small 'get together' tomorrow evening would take place without her.

She said goodbye nicely and, tearing the slip of paper from the notepad, she put it in her pocket and went back to the sitting room.

'You were a long time,' her mother accused her.

'Was I?' Alethea thought she hadn't been speaking with Trent for more than a few minutes.

'What did he want?' Eleanor Pemberton demanded.

Alethea didn't want to tell her. Somehow, she just knew it: the fact that Trent de Havilland had invited her out for a second time would be all her fault.

'He's having a small—er—party tomorrow night. He asked if I'd like to go along.'

'You're not going?' It sounded more of a statement than a question.

Wondering what her mother would do if she said yes—have apoplexy on the spot, she wouldn't wonder—Alethea merely answered with a dutiful, 'No.'

'I should think so. You tell him next time he rings not to bother you again.'

Alethea gave more thought to leaving home as she lay wakeful in her bed that night. Her mother usually kicked up a fuss whenever she asserted her right to go out with someone if she so wished. But, since Trent had called for her last Tuesday, Mother had seemed to carp non-stop.

Alethea knew that her mother had endured a hard time, and she was sorry about that. But, unlike Maxine, who was having trouble getting any maintenance money from Keith, her father had seen to it that his wife kept their house and had a good monthly allowance. Though, thinking about it, her mother would have had lawyers sitting on his doorstep night and day had he attempted to do otherwise.

Alethea stopped herself right there. Grief! She was sounding as bitter as her mother! Quite when her thoughts had become a touch on the sour side, she couldn't have said. But suddenly Alethea knew without question that the time had come for her to cease merely thinking about leaving home. If some of her mother's bitterness wasn't to rub off permanently on to her, she had to do something about it now. The trick would be to find the nerve to tell her mother what she had in mind.

Saturday dawned early. Sadie, with a sleepy-eyed Georgia in tow, came into Alethea's bedroom and woke her up. 'I'm bored,' Sadie announced.

'And me,' Georgia echoed.

'Looks as though we're in for another fun-filled Saturday.' Alethea struggled to sit up. She knew that there was not the remotest likelihood that they were going to allow her to go back to sleep again. 'We could go down and have breakfast,' she suggested.

'*Yes!*' they whooped in unison.

The morning that had started off noisily grew progressively worse. Lunch ended in a pitched battle with Sadie being sent to her room yelling, '*It's not fair!*' and with Georgia smiling cheerfully at the outcome.

Alethea, who had been hoping at some time during the morning to find a tactful way of telling her mother that she had decided to find somewhere else to live, accepted then that she wasn't going to get the chance of a quiet talk until all three of Maxine's offspring were tucked up in bed.

Sadie was unusually silent upstairs. It was a silence Alethea didn't trust. She went upstairs and found Sadie in her bedroom experimenting with her lipsticks.

'Suits you,' she murmured faintly. Guessing they were all in for an afternoon of hell, she added, 'If I can square it with your mother, do you fancy a walk.'

'Past the sweetshop?'

'Into it if you like.'

Only just did Alethea manage to avoid a sudden and impetuous kiss from her heavily lipsticked niece.

Polly was still a little poorly, so it only took half an hour to clean up Sadie and get her and Georgia ready.

In all, Alethea had them out of the house for around three hours. But, at least, thanks to a nearby playground with slides and swings, plus a mile-and-a-half-long ramble, when they returned with sweet bags in hand, they were looking fit, healthy and cheerful, and even managing to talk at a less than high-pitched level.

If the two girls were looking cheerful, however, it was more than could be said for their mother. Maxine looked extremely worried and as if—but for the presence of her daughters—she would be in floods of tears again.

Alethea gave her a questioning look; Maxine shook her head. Clearly she did not wish to discuss the fresh crisis which had presented itself while the children were around. Alethea could make a fair guess at who was at the root of Maxine's present upset, though, when her mother coldly let fall in passing, '*He* called!'

Alethea had to wait until the children were upstairs in bed, and she and Maxine were in the kitchen tidying up, before she heard anything of why Keith Lawrence had that afternoon braved his mother-in-law's house.

He was, it seemed, to be prosecuted. SEC, Trent de Havilland's company, had decided they now had sufficient evidence to have him tried for diverting some of the company's funds into his own bank account.

'Oh, Maxine, I'm so sorry!' Alethea gasped, realising that it hadn't taken the powers that be very long to have a case against her brother-in-law all neatly tied up. 'Is he sure it will come to that—prison, I mean?'

'He's positive,' Maxine answered shakily, adding, in obvious distress, 'We'd just started to agree that any money left over from the sale of the house—once he's paid everything back—I could have. But, unless someone can put in a good word for him, it will mean...' She started to cry. 'It will m-mean that my girls will have to bear the stigma of having a jail-bird for a father. Oh, I can't bear it!'

'Oh, Max, don't...' Her heart was wrung, and Alethea couldn't bear her sister's distress. She left off wiping down the work surfaces and went over to put an arm around Maxine. 'Perhaps it won't come to jail. Perhaps someone *will* speak up for him. Has Keith a friend at work who...?'

'He hasn't been there all that long. He knows no one really, except...' Maxine broke off to wipe her eyes. 'Except, you,' she ended.

For several witless seconds Alethea stared at her. 'Me?' she questioned, smiling nervously as she sought to understand what her sister meant. 'What have I...?'

'You know Trent de Havilland,' Maxine enlightened her.

'Tr...' Alethea's lovely violet eyes widened in alarm as, appalled, comprehension started to dawn. 'Yes, but...' She gasped.

'You could go to his party tonight and, if need be, beg him not to prosecute.' Maxine, it seemed, after hours of worrying, had come up with the only possible solution.

'I couldn't do that!' Alethea argued in a strangled voice.

'Why not?' Maxine wanted to know, sounding tougher than she looked. 'I'd do it for you.'

'Oh, Maxine...' Alethea cried. Her sister's distress was her distress. But surely Maxine could see that Alethea couldn't possibly do what she was asking. 'Trent doesn't even know Keith. He'd have no idea who on earth I was talking about.' She tried to counter Maxine's insane idea with reason.

'He doesn't have to know Keith,' Maxine continued. 'He's the chairman of the whole shoot. All he has to do is pick up the phone and give the order to drop the prosecution and...'

Oh, Heavens! Maxine was seeing her wild notion as perfectly feasible, Alethea could see that she was. 'But Keith *stole* from him!' she cut in to protest.

'And you're his sister-in-law, my sister and aunt to his three children,' Maxine said forcefully. This was her only chance and for her three children she would fight—and expect their aunt to do the same.

'I'm—sorry,' Alethea mumbled, and, unable to bear the accusing look in Maxine's eyes, she left the kitchen and went up to her room, with an unbearable weight of guilt dogging her footsteps.

That same guilt plagued her for another half an hour while she sat on her bed and tried to forget Maxine's tear-stained face. Maxine seemed to think there was nothing to it. That Alethea could just bowl up to Trent's gathering and do as she asked. But how could she?

Another half an hour went by and, wriggle though she might, Alethea, thinking of Maxine tearing herself apart, thinking of Maxine's pronouncement, 'I'd do it for you', found she had presented herself with a new problem: how could she not do it?

She didn't want to do it. No way did she want to do it. The idea of driving over to the smart area where Trent de Havilland lived, of ringing his doorbell and then of somehow or other getting him alone and saying, Oh, by the way... and then confessing she was the sister-in-law of a man who had robbed his company, and going on from there to ask him to stop the prosecution, was utterly and totally ludicrous.

Why should Trent do it? Why should he take any notice, for goodness' sake? He was a businessman, for certain upright in all his dealings, or Hector Chapman would not consider him a friend. So why, in creation, should Trent take any notice of her, someone he barely knew, pleading the case of someone he didn't know, but who had cheated his company?

She glanced at her watch. It was half past nine. She went and had a shower, and was still mentally protesting against what she was doing when she applied powder and lipstick and stepped into the plain mustard-coloured dress she had worn the last time she had seen Trent.

Was it only last Tuesday? It seemed ages ago. With luck she might make it to his home before eleven. Oh, grief, she didn't want to go.

She had her car keys in her hand and was halfway down the stairs when it all at once dawned on her that Maxine could have said nothing to their mother of what she was going to ask Alethea to do. Alethea could quite see why. For, regardless of any stigma Maxine believed would attach itself to the children if their father was sent to prison, his mother-in-law would take only delight from the fact he was having to pay for his misdeeds. Prison, in her mother's opinion, would be the best place for him.

In view of her mother's lack of sympathy, Alethea was positive that Maxine would want her to keep their discussion to herself. That being so, her mother was going to raise the roof when she went into the sitting room to mention she had changed her mind and was just off to Trent de Havilland's party.

The thought of her parent's wrath gave Alethea some moments of unease. But then, perhaps in relation to that word 'sympathy', she recalled thinking that sympathy on its own would not be much help to Maxine.

Time to suit her actions to her sympathy. Alethea took a brave breath and continued down the stairs. 'Where on earth are you going?' her mother demanded the moment she walked through the sitting-room door, spotting at once that her younger daughter no longer wore jeans and a T-shirt, but looked to be on her way out to a party.

'I—er—changed my mind about going to that party,' Alethea dared, not looking at Maxine in case her mother did a two-and-two addition and came up with a correct four.

'You're going to Trenton de Havilland's party?' her mother questioned incredulously.

'I thought I would.'

'Well, I . . .' Her mother started to give full voice—only for once her elder daughter interrupted her.

'Alethea has a right to a life of her own, Mother.' She willingly drew Eleanor Pemberton's fire on herself, and Alethea didn't hang about.

'And a fine mess you've made of yours!' she heard her mother rally as she got over her shock. By then Alethea was negotiating the chest in the hall.

She found the exclusive area where Trent de Havilland lived without any trouble. But she was already brimful of nerves as she parked the car outside, went up stone steps and rang his doorbell.

Oh, how she wanted to run away as she waited. Oh, it would be so easy! But she could not take that way out. For all she had barely glanced at Maxine before leaving, her sister would know that the only reason she had changed her mind about attending this get-together was to do as she had wanted. To ask Trent de Havilland not to prosecute her crooked brother-in-law. Grief, what on earth had ever made her think Trent would listen, much less agree?

Alethea, though her feet were glued to the doorstep, was mentally all set to run away when she heard the sound of someone coming to answer the door. Oh, help her, somebody! Oh, if only she hadn't come.

'Alethea!' Trent, casually dressed, opened the door to her. He was as she remembered him: tall, dark-eyed, dark-haired. 'Come in,' he invited, stepping back to allow her to come by him.

'I—er—didn't bring a boyfriend. Is that all right?' she blurted out in her nervousness.

'Of course,' he replied evenly, and, closing the door, he continued, 'I'm glad you could make it.' And so saying he led the way into a vast, high-ceilinged drawing room.

The floor was thickly carpeted, with a low table separating a couple of matching sofas which flanked a massive stone fireplace. But, having anticipated being shown into a room full of people, or with at least half a dozen other guests, Alethea saw there were none.

'Oh, no, I got the wrong night!' she exclaimed, appalled.

'The fault is all mine,' Trent replied urbanely, his tall length between her and the door as if he read in her eyes that she was ready to bolt.

'Fault?' she echoed.

'My other guests rang from Paris. They flew over for the day,' he explained. 'Unfortunately, their plane is fog-bound, making it impossible for them to get back tonight.' Flew over for the day! This was another world— but Alethea had no time to dwell on it; she was too busy coming to terms with the fact that, by the sound of it, she was Trent's only guest! 'I should have phoned you,' he went on. 'Forgive me that I didn't,' he apologised. 'I was somehow certain you'd no intention of accepting my invitation.'

Was there a question in his voice? Alethea was too embarrassed to be able to tell for sure. 'Hey-ho!' She tried to make light of it, and, skirting round him, she mumbled, 'I'll—er— see you,' and was at the door.

Trent de Havilland, however, was there before her. 'You're not going?' he asked, making it sound as though he sincerely wanted her to stay a little while.

'I— It's gone eleven, and—and...'

'And you don't have to be up early for work in the morning,' he teased, which reminded her of her mother—who on Tuesday had said the reverse of that—which in turn reminded her of her sister.

Oh, Lord! 'That's true,' she agreed while she tried to sort out the conflict going on in her head. She must have had a brainstorm to think for a moment that she could get upright Trent de Havilland to give the order not to prosecute her brother-in-law! Yet, at the same time, what better opportunity to ask him than now? She didn't even have to try and get him alone to have a quiet word with him. There was no one else there! Perhaps within the next few minutes . . .

'You don't sound very sure,' Trent cut through her thoughts.

Hurriedly Alethea got herself together. 'Er—perhaps I might stay for a cup of coffee,' she answered, and unexpectedly felt like smiling. Trent had asked her back to his home for coffee last Tuesday. She had de-clined—now look at her!

She glanced up and saw his eyes were on her mouth. He caught her looking at him, and was not in the slightest way put out. 'You're very beautiful,' he told her. But before she could decide quite how she felt about Trent finding her beautiful, he stated firmly, 'Coffee. Come into the kitchen with me while I make it.'

The kitchen was very up-to-date, with lots of equipment and, like the drawing room, large and high-ceilinged.

'Did you ditch the boyfriend to come here this evening?' Trent asked conversationally as he set about making her a fresh cup of coffee. He had decided to have one himself, she saw, when he got out two cups and saucers.

Mentally wriggling, Alethea thought of what she had to ask him and decided on honesty. 'I didn't have a date tonight,' she answered truthfully. She found the silence that followed deafening. Trent was nobody's fool; he was bound to know that there was more to her turning up the way she had, at this time of night, than any mere acceptance of his invitation. Or was it just her guilty conscience that made her think that?

It was, she realised a moment later. Trent was loading the coffee and cups onto a tray, and, turning to her, those dark eyes seeming to penetrate her very soul, he asked, 'Do I conclude I'm someone special?' He sounded every bit as if he was serious, when she knew he had to be joking.

'In your dreams!' she replied, and laughed—and felt a good deal better when Trent laughed too.

'After you,' he instructed, and followed her to the drawing room with the coffee.

Alethea poured, taking charge of the pot instinctively, and with the low table between them, Trent sitting on a sofa on one side and she perched on the other, the question she had to ask—didn't want to ask—waited for its opportunity.

'Thought any more of finding a place of your own?' Trent kept the conversational ball rolling as they sipped their coffees.

He'd remembered! Though, since he was probably still nursing a bruise on his shin after saying hello to that chest in the hall, she supposed it might be difficult to forget her mentioning the possibility of her leaving home in the same breath as 'overcrowding'.

Alethea looked across at him. 'I'm going to start looking for somewhere next week,' she replied, and knew as she said it, that, come

Monday, she would set about finding a home of her own.

Trent made no comment, but seemed to approve of her decision. But then he confused her totally by stating, when she thought he had forgotten, 'You didn't have a date tonight.' She shook her head, wondering what tack he was on now. 'Do you have a steady man-friend?' he wanted to know.

Did he think she'd be there if she had? 'I've—friends,' she answered, and found herself adding as Trent's gaze stayed steady on her face, 'Though I'm careful not to—' Her breath caught and she abruptly broke off. She barely knew Trent, yet here she was on the way to revealing her innermost secrets to him. 'What have you put in this coffee?' she countered.

'Nothing, I promise you,' he grinned—and Alethea discovered that she found his superb mouth fascinating. She also had to wonder what it was about him that had led her to tell him she was leaving home before she had told her mother, and she had as near as dammit revealed to him her care not to... 'So tell me, Alethea,' he went on smoothly, with not so

much as a hint of what was to come, 'why are
you afraid to commit yo——?'

'I'm not!' she interrupted him in a hurry,
her cup and saucer going down on the table
with a clatter.

'You're afraid to trust,' he stated calmly,
not one bit put out by her agitated manner,
though his eyes on her were alert and
watchful.

'I'm not,' she denied again, hating him and
all scientists in general, who saw what they
thought was a problem and weren't satisfied
until they'd rooted out the cause.

'You trust me, then?'

She looked at him. Of course she didn't
trust him. 'I'm here, aren't I?' she answered
snappily, beginning to feel cross and not
wanting him, with his scientific brain, wondering why she was there when he knew as
well as she that she'd previously had no such
intention. The time wasn't right to tell him,
to ask him, not just now. Unfortunately, in
her attempt to rapidly take the subject away
from why she was there, Alethea latched onto
that word 'trust', and went headlong into
another subject she didn't want to discuss.
'Anyway, I've already told you——' she

changed course in a rush '—my father ran out on us when I was ten!'

'He ran out on your mother,' Trent corrected. 'And you blame him?'

'You obviously don't!' she snapped, and, incensed, she was on her feet. Trent was on his too when she let off another volley: 'And if that isn't enough of an example, my sister was unfortunate enough to fall for a man who was constantly inconstant. You think I should meekly walk in and invite some of the same?'

'Any man who looked at another woman while you were around would want his head examining,' Trent replied, calm when she was going out of control.

'Huh!' she scorned, acting instinctively, with no time to wonder what it was about this man that gave him the power from one instant to the next to cause her to lose her normal equilibrium. She started to move towards the door, and the reason why she was there at all completely went from her mind as she strove for the calm—and courtesy—to tell Trent, 'I'm going.'

Trent had moved too, she found, when she felt the grip of his hand on her arm. 'No, you're not,' he informed her levelly, turning her to face him. 'Calm down,' he instructed evenly, his eyes searching hers.

'I am calm!' she lied, tugging her arm and trying to get free, though to no avail.

Suddenly, in the face of her blatant lie, Trent laughed. She wanted to hit him. 'What you need,' he had the nerve to utter—despite her protest—while he slowly gathered her into his arms, 'is a good cuddle.' She wanted to laugh *and* hit him.

'No, I don't!' she denied heatedly, struggling to get away.

'Relax, Alethea,' he coaxed softly. There was nothing in any way threatening about him. 'Relax, be yourself. Stop mouthing the words you've been spoon-fed at least since your father left home, and, most likely, before he left. Leave home yourself,' he urged. 'Forget most of what your mother has planted in your head. Let the real you through. Learn to trust. To—'

'Have you *quite* finished?' Alethea cut him off.

'Sweetheart,' he replied, 'I haven't yet started.' And, so saying, he gently touched his lips to hers.

Alethea was so startled by his action that for a second she was immobile. Then, abruptly, she jerked back. 'Don't!' she ordered. But he still had her in his arms.

'You kiss me, then,' he suggested, and she would have sworn there was the very devil dancing in his eyes.

'How long can you wait?'

'I'm not going anywhere—I live here,' he hinted softly.

Why did she want to laugh, when she felt so cross? Alethea stared at him, at his good-looking face that was so close. Was he saying that she was going nowhere either, until she had kissed him? This was ridiculous! She glanced to his mouth; it really was quit superb.

She tensed, braced herself, and moved her head a little forward. Then she pulled back nervously and looked into his eyes again. Those dark, calm eyes looked back encouragingly. Again she leaned forward, upward, halted a moment. And then she touched her lips to his.

His mouth was warm, his arms about her were loose now that she had ceased struggling. 'May I go?' she asked, but not angrily, or crossly.

'Of course,' he replied, but continued to hold her, and she looked up into his eyes again and felt most peculiarly no longer in need of breaking free.

'Thank you for the coffee,' she managed, mesmerised.

'Any time you're passing,' he invited.

She laughed, had to, a light laugh that curved her mouth sweetly. She saw his glance stray to her parted lips again, and her laughter died. His gaze returned to her eyes, held them, and she was transfixed once more.

When Trent bent to kiss her, she did not move. His mouth was warm and gentle. He drew her a little closer to him. She put her hands on his waist, but did not pull away.

Trent broke the kiss and brought her nearer to him still. Their bodies touched as he placed tender lips on the side of her neck.

Alethea had no idea when she had stopped protesting. All she knew, as Trent held her in his arms and his lips sought hers again, was that he was stirring an excitement in her that caused her to have problems with her breathing.

She moved her hands from his waist, her arms going a little way around him. When he kissed her once more, she held onto him, her heart racing.

Somehow, and she had not the smallest recollection how, she found she was sitting on a sofa with him. 'Sweet Alethea,' he murmured, but when he went to gently ease her into lying down, suddenly some stray realisation of what she was doing managed to get through.

She resisted. Stiffened in his arms. Became aware, and pulled back, striving hard not to panic. 'I...' was all she was capable of saying, the word coming out huskily in a voice that did not sound like her own.

Trent stared into her panic-filled eyes. 'Don't look so worried,' he murmured, and gently, but very briefly, he placed a light kiss on her mouth. Then, drawing back again, he stated, 'My dear, if it's not your intention to spend this night with me, may I suggest I see you to your car?'

'Where did I put my car keys?' she answered, and didn't know quite how she felt when Trent looked amused. He wasn't about to try and pressure her into his bed?

Nor did he try again to persuade her as he saw her into her car. He waved to her as she drove off, and the last she saw of him was through her rear-view mirror; Trent was standing on the pavement watching her.

She turned the corner and he went from her view. She had been driving for all of two minutes before she realised that she had the stupidest of smiles on her face.

Two minutes after that, however, and her smile abruptly departed. Only then did she realise that she had gone to Trent's home with the express purpose of asking him not to prosecute her brother-in-law, and, in the end, she had done nothing of the sort!

Oh, Heavens! Alethea quickly considered her options. They were few. But one thing was for certain. No way, after Trent had intimated that he would quite enjoy spending the night with her, could she go back and present herself on his doorstep!

CHAPTER FOUR

ALETHEA opened her eyes on Sunday and promptly closed them again. She was not ready to start this day. Yet she was plagued by memories of last night, and to go back to sleep again was an impossibility.

Trent de Havilland had kissed her last night. And she had kissed him back. Even now, as daybreak gave way to morning light, Alethea found that she had to swallow as she recalled his gentle kisses, demanding her response. Yet somehow he had been undemanding of her. Somehow he had been more giving than taking.

Oh, rot, she scorned a moment later, and deliberately turned her thoughts away from Trent de Havilland and instead to how she had flicked the hall light on when she'd got home only to very nearly jump out of her skin as she saw Maxine, who had been sitting on the stairs waiting in the darkness for her return.

'Let's go into the kitchen,' Maxine had whispered, and Alethea's heart had sunk. Plainly she wanted to hear how things had gone! Equally plainly, she did not want to disturb either her daughters or her mother by discussing the matter in the hallway.

'Hot chocolate?' Alethea suggested once they were in the kitchen—a delaying tactic, nothing more.

Maxine clearly had other things on her mind and impatiently shook her head. 'What did he say?'

All too obviously her sister was suffering, and Alethea felt dreadful. 'I...' she began to confess, but at the look of strain on Maxine's face it just seemed beyond her to own up that Trent had the power to make her so cross she forgot everything, that he had the power to so confuse her she had no chance to remember why she had gone to the 'party' after all. And nothing on this earth would have her telling anyone, even her sister, how, when Trent had started to kiss her, they had somehow moved from a standing position to be seated, wrapped in each other's arms on a sofa, without her being in any way aware of having moved a step. 'I wasn't able to ask him,' Alethea blurted out hurriedly.

'Oh, Alethea!' Maxine cried disappointedly. 'Because of the other people there?'

Maxine sounded so forlorn that Alethea just could not tell her the truth. She felt as wretched as her sister looked when she grabbed at the excuse Maxine had given her. 'It just—wasn't convenient—with everybody there,' she lied. But when Maxine looked as though she might break down in floods of tears at any moment, she heard herself add to her lie, 'I'm seeing him again on Monday; I'll ask him then.'

'Oh, would you? I'll never forget this!' Maxine exclaimed.

Alethea had gone up to bed incredulous that, in that weak moment of not wanting her sister to be any more upset than she already was, she had said what she had.

Alethea was still feeling incredulous when, after her restless night, she faced the fact that, whether she was ready to start this Sunday or not, she was too het up to stay in bed any longer.

She showered and dressed and went downstairs to the kitchen, knowing that she was going to have to confess her lie to Maxine at some time during the day. She could not let her go on a minute longer than necessary in the false hope that her husband might not after all be prosecuted.

Alethea made a pot of tea and automatically poured her mother a cup. She took it upstairs, reasoning that Maxine would probably have had a better night's sleep. She would certainly be less tearful, and looking more able to cope, Alethea decided as she went quietly into her mother's room.

'What time did you get in last night?' her mother demanded. She was already awake, and full of acid by the sound of it, and all before Alethea could take the cup and saucer from the tray and place it down on the bedside table.

'I wasn't late,' she replied calmly.

'I suppose we can count ourselves favoured that you deigned to come home at all,' her mother charged with spiteful sarcasm. On top of everything else, Alethea just did not need this. 'After all I've told you about men, that you should so blatantly ignore...'

Her mother's tirade seemed to go on non-stop and suddenly Alethea had had enough.

She supposed she had been coming to the boil for some while. It had nothing to do with her having met Trent de Havilland, or his urgings that she leave home, she was sure. But when her mother got to the part about Alethea treating her home like some hotel—totally unfairly, in Alethea's view, since apart from going to her office she so seldom went out—something in her snapped.

'Actually, Mother, you won't have to worry about me treating this place like a hotel for much longer. I intend looking for somewhere else to live tomorrow.'

For once her mother was so stunned she was silenced. Alethea went back downstairs amazed that it had been so easy. She had thought she would have to lead up to leaving home gently. To tentatively suggest that, if her mother wouldn't mind, and because they were all living on top of each other since Maxine and the children had arrived, she thought she might move out. But it hadn't happened like that. No tentative lead-ups, or anything like that. Just a bald statement of fact: 'I intend looking for somewhere else to live tomorrow'. And that was that!

Oh, would that it were *that* easy. Her announcement that she was going had been. But there was still the whole of that Sunday to be got through. It was not going to be a happy day.

Alethea sorely needed to get Maxine alone so she might own up to lying about seeing Trent on Monday. She realised that her chances of doing that were going to be slender when her mother appeared in the breakfast room at about the same time as Maxine and the girls, and she was made very aware that today was going to be 'Get at Alethea Day'.

'Did your sister tell you that she is leaving us?' Eleanor Pemberton addressed her elder daughter.

'You're leaving?' Maxine asked, looking at Alethea in surprise.

'I thought I'd like to try living in a flat of my own,' Alethea answered, and found she spent most of the rest of the day having to defend her decision. The only bright spot came when Sadie, totally unaware of the strained atmosphere, piped up to ask, practically, if she could have Aunty Alethea's room when she moved out.

The day's miseries were added to when Polly, who had been quite angelic for most of the day—a sign they should have noticed, but didn't, because she was likely to give them hell later to make up for it—started to scream blue murder around six o'clock, and kept it up as only she could.

In consequence, Maxine had her work cut out with Polly, which squashed any last-minute chance Alethea had of having a few words alone with her before she went to bed. When Polly finally went to sleep, from sheer exhaustion, Maxine said she was turning in too.

Alethea spent another worrying night. Any euphoria she might have felt after she had actually told her mother of her intention to leave was negated by the worry that she had lied to Maxine and had done nothing to set that right.

Nor was she able to do anything the next morning. Because, just as she was leaving the house ready to go to work, an anxious slippered and housecoat-clad Maxine came out onto the drive.

'You didn't say what time you were meeting Trent de Havilland today. Whether it was for lunch or dinner. But I just wanted to urge you, if it's for lunch, to do your best for me, Alethea, won't you?'

Alethea opened her mouth. 'I...' she attempted. The words stuck. 'It won't be for the want of trying,' she found herself assuring her sister.

Taking a picture of Maxine's pleading expression with her, Alethea drove to her office, aware now—as she had most likely been yesterday, only she had kicked against admitting it then—that at some time before this day was over she was going to have to try and make contact with Trent de Havilland.

She felt sick inside as she went into her office and began opening the day's post. 'Are you all right?' Carol Robinson asked as they went through the mail together. 'You seem worried.'

'I'm fine,' Alethea stated brightly, but knew that, as the prospect of what she had to do grew larger and larger by the minute, she was going to have to take some action sooner rather than later.

She waited until Carol went in to see Mr Chapman, knowing that Carol would be with him for about a half an hour and that she

would have the office to herself. Then she
found the telephone number she needed in the
private address book Carol kept for Mr
Chapman, and put through her call.

'SEC. Good morning,' answered an ef-
ficient-sounding voice.

'Mr de Havilland's PA, please,' Alethea
requested.

'One moment, please.'

Alethea did not have to wait long before
another voice answered. She took a steadying
breath, 'Is that Mr de Havilland's PA?' she
asked.

'Mrs Tustin's in with Mr de Havilland just
now. May I take a message?'

So far, it had been relatively uncompli-
cated. Now was not the time to have second
thoughts! 'Oh, dear, it's rather urgent I speak
with either Mrs Tustin or Mr de Havilland.
I'm Alethea Pemberton of Mr Hector
Chapman's office. Gale Drilling International,' she added for a little extra clout.
'Is it at all possible you could put me through,
do you think?'

'It's urgent, you said?'

No time to swallow or wonder if what she
was doing—using her employer's name—was

a dismissable offence. 'Extremely,' she said firmly.

'Would you hold, please?'

Alethea had no time either in which to feel relieved that she was actually going to be put through to Trent's PA, for, before she was ready for it: 'Alethea?' queried the voice she would know anywhere.

'Trent,' she answered—and just didn't know where to go from there.

The silence stretched as he waited for her to announce her business, but her throat had dried. 'You have something extremely urgent to discuss?' Trent waited no longer; clearly he was a very busy man.

Alethea took a gulp of breath, and plunged in, 'I n-need to see you rather urgently, if you can spare me a few minutes of your time?' she said in a rush—and died a thousand deaths in the small silence that followed.

'On a business matter?' Trent questioned crisply, and Alethea knew then that he had her measure. Any business would be done directly with her employer. By no chance would a man in Trent de Havilland's position have business discussions with any assistant PA, no matter whose office she worked in.

'S-sort of,' she stammered; it was obvious by then, anyway. 'But not Mr Chapman's business.' She took a steadying breath. 'It's—er—sort of—personal business.' Rushing straight on while her nerve lasted, she went on, 'Could I see you today, do you think?'

'It does sound urgent,' he commented, and Alethea's hopes grew when it sounded as if Trent was pausing to consult his desk diary, because there followed a few moments of silence. Then he was back with her once more, his voice authoritative and decisive. 'There's a park near you. I'll be passing on my way to an appointment just after midday. You're sure this will only take a few minutes?'

'Certain,' Alethea replied. Shortly afterwards she put down her phone and ran the whole gamut of emotions.

She felt panicky inside at what she had to ask him. Nervous and sick. And yet, at the same time—when she knew full well that if Trent's work was anywhere near as hectic as Mr Chapman's, he barely had a moment spare in his day—she also felt slightly rebellious at his intimation that if this was going to take more than a few minutes, she could forget it.

He hadn't said that on Saturday night, when he'd intimated he wasn't averse to taking her to his bed, had he? Alethea abruptly switched her mind away from such thoughts—*this was business*. Well, sort of. And she should be grateful, not mutinous, that, probably on his way to some high-powered lunch, Trent had agreed to stop by the park for a few minutes. She should be grovelling at his feet that he was sparing her his time, not feeling irked that he was condescending to let her have those few minutes.

Pride and panic had a lot to do with how she felt, she realised. Pride that insisted that she simply could not ask him what she had to. Panic that, the question asked, he would castigate her for her nerve. But, whatever the outcome, Alethea now knew that ask she would. The die was cast; for Maxine's sake she would go through with it.

The easiest of her problems, in what was a busy day, was having to disrupt the smooth running of the office by changing her lunch hour. 'It's a business matter,' she explained to Carol.

'You're not going for an interview for another job, are you?' Carol asked quickly, flatteringly, and plainly not caring for the idea.

'Nothing at all like that,' Alethea promised.

'In that case, change your lunch hour with my blessing,' Carol smiled. 'If it's anything I can help with?' she offered. 'You were looking worried earlier.'

'No, it's all right. Nothing I can't cope with,' Alethea assured her cheerfully—oh, that it was so simple!

Work went on at its usual speedy rate while the hands on her watch alternately crawled and galloped. There was a brief respite around eleven, when Ralph King from Marketing came in with a fair-haired man in his late twenties and introduced him as one of their new executives.

Both Alethea and Carol shook hands with Nick Saunders, but it was to Alethea he looked when he remarked, 'I'm sure I'm going to be very happy here.'

'Another one bites the dust,' Carol teased when the two men had gone. 'But I don't suppose you'll go out with him either,' she added, referring to the fact that, though she had many offers, Alethea made a policy of never dating anyone from work.

'He won't ask,' Alethea answered lightly.

'Ten pounds!' Carol jokingly laid the bet, and they both laughed, and got on with some work.

Inside a minute Alethea had forgotten all about Nick Saunders. Though it could not be said that she was concentrating all her thoughts on the work in front of her. Just in case Trent was early she'd start to get ready around eleven-thirty.

Alethea was at the park gates at eleven-fifty, her insides jumbled by barely controlled panic as she rehearsed and rehearsed what she had to say in the least ghastly way.

Her panic was in no way helped when twelve o'clock came and went with no sign of Trent. Nor was he there at one minute past twelve or two minutes past twelve. She knew, because she could not stop checking her watch.

At five minutes past twelve, a limousine drew up. Trent got out and Alethea's heart went into overdrive. She wrestled with her nerves as Trent, in his immaculate dark business suit, crisp shirt and silk tie, and looking every tall inch of what he was—a most successful business-man—instructed his chauffeur to wait.

He spotted Alethea at once and came striding over. He greeted her and, barely pausing in his stride, a man brimful of energy, placed a hand beneath her elbow and escorted her inside the park to a nearby bench. He waited until they were both seated, then turned to look at her; the floor was all hers!

'Thank you for agreeing to see me,' she opened, her rehearsed speech forgotten as dark, all-seeing eyes scrutinised her.

'What can I do for you?' he helped her out.

Oh, Heavens, this was dreadful. Every bit as dreadful as she had imagined it would be. 'The thing is...' She paused and coughed to clear a suddenly dry throat. 'The thing is...' she began again.

'The thing is?' Trent was there again to help her out. Or maybe, several minutes having already gone, he was impatient for her to spell out her difficulties so that he could get to his appointment. 'You have a personal business problem you want my help with, but don't know where to begin?' He stated the case most aptly, though why that should niggle her she didn't know. But it did. 'Why not start at the beginning?' he suggested logically.

Had he got that long? The idea made Alethea strive harder to get her words said. If she didn't buck her ideas up, his patience would be at an end and he would be gone. Thoughts of going home and seeing Maxine that evening with nothing accomplished spurred her on.

'Well, to begin with, it's more to do with my sister and the—er—predicament she's in than me.'

'Interesting,' he observed.

She forced herself to go on. 'Apparently her husband . . .'

'Is she still separated from him?'

'There's little likelihood of a reconciliation,' Alethea stated.

'Go on,' Trent instructed, when she came to a full stop again.

Alethea coughed nervously, and revealed in a rush, 'Keith—Maxine's husband—works for you. Or did.'

'Did?'

'He—er—must have worked in some section that deals with money. It . . .' Oh, Lord, 'It seems he may have borrowed some.'

Trent de Havilland, as she already knew, was nobody's fool. His look was uncompromising when he stated, more than asked, 'With no intention of paying it back.'

'He's put their house up for sale and means to repay the money,' Alethea said quickly. 'But until it's sold Maxine doesn't have any money either.' Not pausing for breath, and having got started, she rushed on, 'But, worse than that, Maxine can't bear the thought of the stigma for her daughters if Keith goes to prison—as she believes he certainly will.'

'We're prosecuting?' Trent asked; as she had suspected, he had managers who dealt with that sort of thing, without bothering him with the details.

'Yes. Keith was suspended initially, but...'

'The case against him must be indisputable,' Trent interrupted. She had realised that for herself, and nodded, not feeling any better. Trent looked at her for long moments, his expression stern. 'You knew all of this when you went out with me last Tuesday?' he asked shortly.

'No!' she promptly denied. 'I knew Keith worked at some place called SEC and that he'd been suspended. But I'd no idea then that you were anything to do with the company, or its chairman. I would never have gone out with you had I known!'

Trent made a sound which gave Alethea not the slightest clue as to how he had taken her answer. But he was as shrewd as ever when, in the same stern tone, he questioned, 'But you knew on Saturday when you came to my home?'

'Yes,' she had to confess. 'But you had invited me . . .'

'That,' he returned shortly, 'had little to do with why you came. The only reason for your arriving at my door was your brother-in-law.'

'Yes,' she agreed miserably, and found herself confessing, 'I'd made up my mind not to see you again—which I think you knew. Oh, I realised you weren't bothered about that,' she rushed on quickly, feeling a little pink about the cheeks. 'That much was obvious, when you suggested I bring a boyfriend along. Anyhow . . .' She sensed she was going off at a tangent, and made herself slow down. 'Anyway, Maxine knew about your invitation, and after Keith had called on Saturday afternoon, to tell her that SEC had decided to prosecute, she begged me—and I was most reluctant, honestly—to come and see you.'

'To accept my invitation?'

'We thought I might be able to have a quiet word with you,' she admitted, not feeling one whit better for doing so. Who said confession was good for the soul? 'Only...'

'Only—my other guests were fog-bound in Paris but, when you had ample opportunity to plead your brother-in-law's case, you did not.'

'You kissed me!' Alethea blurted out. She went scarlet and stood up. 'You confuse me!' she exclaimed agitatedly, turning her back on him. He rose to his feet too. Because she had solved nothing, she felt forced to turn around again. 'Will you?' she asked.

'Will I what?'

Damn him, he knew what she was asking! But she forced herself to go on. 'Will you consider not prosecuting Keith Lawrence?' she asked.

Trent's answer was to stare down into her unhappy violet eyes. Several seconds elapsed. 'I'll look into it,' was the most he would promise. 'I'll be in touch,' he added and, to her astonishment, he bent down, placed a light kiss on her cheek, straightened and strode briskly away.

Alethea stared after him, her left hand going to her left cheek. There had been no time for her to react, object, move away or do anything. Why, though, had he kissed her cheek in—friendly—farewell? She went and had a cup of coffee.

Alethea had given up trying to fathom why Trent de Havilland did what he did when she went back to her office. She was fairly positive she had been pleading a lost cause when she had asked him to intervene in her brother-in-law's prosecution. But had she? That kiss to her cheek, light though it had been, made her hope.

Trent had said he would look into it and would be in touch. How soon? Would he ring her at the office? He must know, surely, how anxious she was to hear his decision.

She was jumpy all that afternoon. Each time the phone on her desk rang her mouth went dry, but it was never Trent. She stayed at the office a little after five, rather than miss his call if it came through.

He did not ring. Alethea drove home realising that he had probably been much too busy that day to find time to investigate the details of the case.

'Well, did you find somewhere?' her mother asked her acidly, when she arrived home.

'Find...' Alethea began, her thoughts so taken up with the lack of news she had to pass to her sister that she did not at once understand the question.

'You said you were leaving,' her young niece, Sadie, piped up.

It was no wonder to Alethea that she had forgotten her intention to start looking for somewhere else to live that day. 'Not yet,' she answered her mother pleasantly. 'I'll go up and change.'

Sadie had been into her room and deposited several of her dolls on her bed, Alethea noted as she changed into jeans and a white shirt. By the look of it, the little love couldn't wait for Alethea to be gone so she could take full possession of her room.

Alethea was about to go downstairs, ready to give a hand with dinner or children, whichever was the greater priority, when Maxine, with Polly on her hip, took the chance to have a private word.

'Was it lunch?' she asked. This time Alethea understood the question at once.

'He's going to get in touch as soon as he's found out more about it,' was the best Alethea could tell her.

'But you did ask him?'

'Oh, yes.' Alethea wished she could be more encouraging, but dared not, lest Maxine was in for crushing disappointment.

'How did he seem to t...?' Her voice tailed off when their mother called up the stairs that Georgia was fighting with Sadie. 'Are you *certain* you want to settle for a career?' Maxine asked whimsically, and somehow both of them managed to find a smile.

It had been one of those days, apparently, and dinner was a scratch of a meal. None of the girls wanted to go to bed but, with bribery, corruption and, in the end, extreme crossness, Maxine at last got Sadie and Georgia up the stairs.

Her sister was still upstairs, reading the girls a story, Alethea realised, as she walked the floor downstairs with a pyjama-clad Polly. She was singing softly to the tot, when someone rang the doorbell.

Alethea glanced towards her mother, but saw she was not prepared to take over Polly while she went to answer the door, so Alethea took the little girl with her.

Her guess was that it was someone collecting jumble for the scouts. She pulled back the door, expecting to look downwards to some youngster, and found she had to look up.

'Trent!' she exclaimed, and felt instantly confused. She hadn't been expecting him to call—hadn't so much as given that possibility a thought. Oh, grief, her white shirt bore liberal traces of Polly's chocolate pudding— after a hurried wipe with a wet cloth; that had been a mistake!

'Hello, cherub,' Trent answered, and she knew he was talking to Polly, who beamed at him in pure delight.

'You've put her in a good mood. She's been a monster for most of the evening.'

'It's an effect I have on women,' he replied easily. 'Coming for a drive?' he asked.

This was it! Alethea was worried. Why did she have to go for a drive? Was it bad news? How could it be good? If it was good news, surely he would have said by now, or even have picked up the phone.

'Y-yes,' she replied nervously, realising that, whatever news he had, he did not want to discuss it over the phone. 'Er—I'll have to change my shirt. Will you come in?' she invited belatedly.

'I'll wait in the car,' he said decisively, and she stared at him.

'You're frightened of my mother!' She heard herself accuse him, and couldn't help but wonder what it was about him that sent her brains scattering. What a crass thing to have said!

But Trent didn't seem to think her remark crass. In fact, the corners of his mouth tugged up pleasantly at the corners. 'Terrified,' he agreed, and walked away to his car.

Alethea found she was smiling as she closed the door. Abruptly she sobered. This wasn't funny. Knowing that if she did not want to suffer a third degree it would be better to hand Polly over to Maxine rather than ask her mother, Alethea went upstairs.

She found Maxine just closing the door on the girls' room. 'Trent's here. He wants to take me for a drive,' she explained in an undertone.

Maxine caught on at once. 'Here, give Polly to me,' she said, taking the two-year-old from her sister.

Alethea was aware that 'a drive' was another phrase for what was about to take place. Clearly Trent had investigated but did not want to tell her his conclusions in her home. With Georgia and Sadie creating the last time he'd called, the house had probably sounded like Bedlam.

After quickly changing into a fresh shirt— they were most likely only going to sit in his car around the corner—Alethea washed her hands and ran a comb through her hair, and strove for calm.

She went back down the stairs realising that she should thank him because he had been so quick in getting back to her. But there was also every chance that she would have nothing to thank him for at the end of it.

She did not want to go into the sitting room to tell her mother where she was going, but felt that while she was living in the same house she owed Eleanor Pemberton that courtesy.

Maxine, she discovered with a touch of relief, had already informed their mother that Alethea was going for a drive with Trent de Havilland. 'This is getting a bit frequent, isn't it?' Eleanor questioned coldly.

Twice! Trent had called at the house twice! If she hadn't known before, Alethea knew then that her decision to move out was the right one. Sadly she realised that her mother was never going to lighten up. Perhaps she had been born that way. But, whatever the facts, Alethea was more sure than ever that she did not want to grow to be like her.

'I shouldn't be too long,' she answered, and made her escape.

Trent got out of his car to open the passenger door the moment she appeared. 'That was quick,' he observed.

Alethea got in, wondering if she'd been too quick, wondering if he realised how anxious she was to hear what he had to tell her. But, most of all, she considered that the whole wretched affair was a nightmare.

They did not merely go around the corner, as she had thought they might, but Trent drove out into open country. He had little to say, and, since all Alethea wanted to speak of was the decision he must have made, she had little to say either. She felt nervous of asking him point-blank what conclusion he had come to, though she came close many times.

The summer evening had given way to dusk when, in a quite picturesque area, with not a house or building in sight, Trent slowed his car and pulled off the road. This was it! This was what she was waiting to hear. She prayed that it would be good news for Maxine and her daughters, and even started to believe that it might be. Trent wouldn't have brought her all this way just to tell her no, would he?

'I thought you might find it pleasant out here after a day in the city,' Trent commented, switching off the engine and turning to her.

That wasn't what she wanted to hear. 'It is—very pleasant,' she agreed.

'You said, on Saturday, that you were going to start looking for somewhere else to live today,' he commented.

What had that got to do with the price of moth balls? 'I've been—er—a little busy!' she hinted.

'Ah, yes,' he commented, as if he had only just remembered. 'You looked rather gorgeous with that child in your arms.'

'Are you being deliberately perverse?' she erupted, her nerves getting the better of her, and groaned in despair. She was asking a tremendous favour of him, she just could not afford to get angry. 'I'm sorry,' she apologised primly. 'I meant I'd been busy arranging to see you—at—at lunchtime, not, as you seem to think, busy helping Maxine with the children.'

Trent stared into her anxious violet eyes. 'Is it hell?' he queried quietly, and she was unsure what he meant. Did he mean the onslaught of three, though quite often most loveable at other times boisterous, screaming, fighting, raising-hell children when she enjoyed peace and quiet? And that was without taking into account that she also lived with a complaining mother and a dear, though frequently tearful sister? Or did he mean it was hell waiting for him to reveal if he was prepared to grant her, on so short an acquaintance, the one very big favour she had asked of him?

She could hold back no longer. 'What have you decided?' she asked solemnly.

'About Keith Lawrence helping himself to money that doesn't belong to him?'

'He'll pay it back. He's ready to, as soon as he can sell the house,' she assured him quickly.

'And you think that that's good enough, when he was in a highly trusted position?'

Alethea felt miserable, and as if she was being challenged to defend her brother-in-law. But how could she? He'd treated Maxine shabbily, and was a thief into the bargain. 'I don't want to argue about it, Trent,' she stated unhappily, staring down at her lap. 'I just want to know what you've decided so—'

'Don't look so sad,' he cut in, and startled her by placing a gentle hand beneath her chin, tilting up her face so he could see into her eyes. 'I've decided,' he began without further ado, 'subject to certain conditions, to give the instruction to cancel the prosecution proceedings.'

'Oh, Trent!' Alethea exclaimed barely before he'd finished. 'Thank you so much! Keith will agree to any conditions you say; I know he w—' Something in Trent's eyes, his look, caused her to break off. 'What...?' she began, and, as Trent took his hand from beneath her chin, she began to feel wary.

She was right to feel so, she discovered a very few moments later, when, without a glimmer of a smile, Trent announced, 'Not Keith Lawrence, Alethea—you.'

'Me!' she echoed, desperately seeking to comprehend. Hurriedly she went back over what had just been said. 'The—er—certain conditions—they apply to me, not my brother-in-law?' was the best she could come up with. An accurate statement, she was made to realise, in next to no time.

'You're the one who asked for my intervention,' Trent pointed out. Well, yes, that was true, but not for herself! 'Once everything between us is agreed upon, and I give instructions about Lawrence, I want his connection with the company ended completely.'

Alethea could appreciate that. Keith had cheated his employer, and in Trent's view there was no room in his firm for a man who could so misuse the trust placed in him. But Trent had said, intimated, that he would only give the word for that prosecution to be scrapped, once 'everything' between them had been agreed upon.

'Between *us*?' she questioned, realising that Trent was watching and waiting while she digested what he said. 'You want me to do something?' she asked, and, in her innocence, actually smiled. 'Well, of course— anything you say,' she offered. Just then, all she could see was Maxine's tremendous peace of mind at knowing that her daughters were not to have a jail-bird for a father.

'Oh, Alethea. You're too much!' Trent exclaimed, somewhat obscurely in her view.

'What did I do?'

'You've just committed yourself without having the first notion of what it is I want.'

'Well, it can't be all that bad,' she answered, cheerful in her relief that, given some condition or other, Trent was going to grant her this enormous favour. 'What is it you want me to do?' she asked, and very nearly fainted when he told her.

His eyes raked her face for long, long moments, before finally, he said, 'I want you to come and live with me.'

Alethea stared at him. His words had penetrated her brain, but she didn't believe them. He held her glance. 'You're...' She coughed. 'You're not—serious?' she managed.

'I was never more so,' he responded evenly.

'No!' she said promptly.

'Think about it.'

'I don't need to,' she told him coldly.

He shrugged. 'Fine,' he accepted, and turned, ready to start up his car.

'*Wait!*' Some of her initial shock was departing, and some sense of what was at stake was starting to penetrate. Trent took his hand off the ignition key and Alethea tried hard to concentrate her thoughts on which was the greater issue here.

It did not matter too much to her that her brother-in-law could go to jail for his misdeeds, but it mattered to her that her sister and nieces might suffer for it. Oh, Lord, had she thought nightmare? Nightmares were easier!

'Why?' she asked chokily, and saw Trent looked amused.

'Don't you *know* that you're a very desirable woman?' he asked.

Oh, grief! She swallowed. 'You mean—er—live with you, with—er—bed, and everything?' she asked.

Trent eyed her steadily. 'Everything,' he confirmed.

'But—but...' Oh, Heavens. This wasn't happening! Say it wasn't happening! To *her*! 'But I don't want to go to bed with you!' she cried in panic.

'You don't have to.' Her heart leapt in relief, until he added two ghastly words: 'Straight away.'

Oh, grief! Her brain seemed befuddled. 'You're saying—that you'll—um—wait?' she managed at last.

'I'll wait,' he answered quietly. No, no, no, screamed her head. 'Look at it this way,' he suggested pleasantly. 'You intend looking for somewhere to live other than your present abode. What's wrong with my place?'

His place was wonderful, absolutely superb. The only trouble was, *he* was in it! 'When I said I'd start looking for somewhere else, it wasn't in my mind to consider sharing,' she commented shakily.

'I'm away a great deal,' he enlightened her matter-of-factly. 'I doubt you'd see a lot of me.' One could only hope! She remembered how only last Friday Trent had returned from Italy. Perhaps he went abroad every week.

It was starting to sound better. Trent away. Trent saying he would wait. Which meant that he wouldn't rush her. She liked him, of course she did. But... oh, Heavens.

'You know I've never been to bed with a man before!' she blurted out in a panicky rush.

Trent seemed as if he had already suspected as much, and as she recalled how he had accused her of being afraid to commit, to trust, so his look softened. 'Have you not, love?' he murmured gently, so gently that hope rose in her that he was going to say, Forget the whole idea. Fat chance! Then, as if he felt some lightness was called for, he smiled, and promised, 'In that case, my dear, you're in for something of a treat!'

Her lips twitched, she couldn't stop them, but she wouldn't smile at his audacity. Rather, she'd prefer to hit him with something blunt and painful. Though, on thinking about it, something sharp and head-splitting would be better.

'Since it seems I'm to consider sharing,' she began acidly, 'would I have my own room?'

'Until such time you wanted to move into mine,' he replied calmly.

'But you'll wait? You said you'd wait?' she asked, panic starting to attack again.

'You have my word,' Trent answered gravely—and strangely, when what he was suggesting was so worrying, she felt she *could* trust him.

A long, long, unbroken silence followed, while Alethea sought for calm and searched every avenue she could for a way out. Only to come to the conclusion that they were all cul-de-sacs. She wanted Trent to halt Keith Lawrence's prosecution. He would, on the condition that she went to live with him. And at some later date she was to join him in his bed.

She sighed heavily. It broke the silence. 'May I think about it?' She grabbed at his earlier suggestion.

He reached for the ignition and had one last thing to say to her before he set the car in motion. 'Don't take too long,' he advised. 'The lawyers are baying for your brother-in-law's blood!'

CHAPTER FIVE

SLEEP was elusive for most of that night. No sooner had she fallen asleep than it seemed to Alethea that she was awake again—with the same problem looming as large as ever.

She had to admit she had not been feeling too affable towards Trent when he'd dropped her off at her door. He had got out of the car and come round to her side, and she'd managed a brief, 'Goodnight'. She had found herself looking up at him. Then, without a word, making not the smallest attempt to persuade her one way or another, without a goodnight, even, he had turned away and she had gone indoors.

Both her mother and sister had still been downstairs, her mother looking particularly spleenish, while Maxine's eyes had been full of questioning.

'Anyone want a warm drink?' Alethea had asked, feeling suddenly a very great need to be on her own.

Maxine had followed her out to the kitchen. 'What happened? What did he say?' she questioned in an urgent undertone—only to find that her mother had come out to the kitchen too.

'What are you two whispering about?' she wanted to know accusingly.

'Nothing secret,' Maxine recovered. 'I was just telling Alethea that I've given up sugar and not to put any in my chocolate.'

'Fads!' her mother snorted, but, it was as if she was convinced that there was some secret here to which she was not privy, because she stayed with them, giving them no opportunity for any private conversation that night.

Dawn crept over the sky and Alethea was awake again. She was quite glad that there had been no chance of a private chat with Maxine. How could she have told her of the price Trent de Havilland had asked? She was very much troubled that her reluctance to confide in Maxine might stem from an uncertainty that Maxine might urge her to go ahead and do this thing, if not for her, then for her three little girls.

Oh, Heavens! Desperately Alethea tried for a solution. Tried to see this problem and its answer logically. Problem: Trent wanted her to move in with him. Logic: she, as he had reminded her, was looking for somewhere else to live.

Abruptly she scrapped logical thinking; she didn't like the answers it brought. And, anyway, there was more to it than that. Trent didn't want her to merely move into his house, he wanted her to move into his bed! At that emotion-tearing thought, Alethea promptly left her own bed and began her day.

She was downstairs pouring out a couple of cups of tea when Maxine found her in the kitchen. Oh, crumbs, she had nothing ready to tell her!

'I've just spent the most ghastly night of my life,' Maxine informed her. Tell me about it! thought Alethea. 'I nearly came into your room at four this morning. But for disturbing Polly...' She did not finish the sentence; she was in a hurry to find out if her husband was going to be prosecuted or not. 'Tell me you've got some good news for me and my girls,' she implored.

'Maxine, I—' Alethea broke off, noticing the dark shadows under her sister's eyes that said more than words about the sleepless nights she had suffered. And, horror-struck, she heard her voice add, 'He isn't going to prosecute.'

'Alethea!' Maxine squealed, so great was her relief.

Alethea stared at her; had she actually told her that Trent de Havilland was not going to prosecute Keith Lawrence? Maxine grabbed hold of her and gave her a very big hug of thanks. Apparently, Alethea realised, she had!

Alethea was stuck in traffic on her way to work when she started to realise the enormity of what she had done. So great was Maxine's relief that years had seemed to slip away from her. So how, then, Alethea wondered, could she unsay it? She couldn't, she realised. Which meant that she would have to go through with it.

Traffic started moving again, and Alethea, giving automatic attention to her driving, wished and wished and wished that she had never ever told Trent de Havilland that she was on the look-out for somewhere else to live.

Wretched man! Wretched idea! She wouldn't do it, she wouldn't! But what about Maxine and the girls? Well, she wasn't going to get into bed with him, that was for sure!

Suddenly Alethea started to feel a little brighter. No way was she going to bed with him. And, since he had said he would wait for that momentous happening, then, since it wasn't going to happen, he would get fed up with waiting, change his mind about wanting her to live with him, and tell her she was free to go.

Of course, she would have to be sure he would keep his word and not prosecute Keith Lawrence. But since she would be keeping her word by going to live with him, she would not be breaking her promise. Trent would do it for her, by telling her he didn't want her living with him any more.

Alethea started to panic a little when she thought to question whether Trent would keep his word? He'd made no bones about telling her he thought her a very desirable woman. Quickly she pushed the thought that he desired her from her mind.

But then she found she was remembering last Saturday evening. He had kissed her, and... She urgently brought her thoughts away from where they were going. Good grief, anyone would think she had desired him, and she hadn't.

Oh, so all right, she had enjoyed his kisses, but they hadn't amounted to very much, not really, and whether Trent had desired her or whether he hadn't, she instinctively knew he was not the sort of man who would force her against her will.

Alethea reflected how she had just dived into an area where she had not wanted to go. But, having done so, she had been able to get it clear in her head that Trent would get fed up with waiting and ask her to leave before he would force her to share his bed.

That being so, she would move in with him. It was a bonus that he was often away, and she would sit it out. While, at the same time, she would start looking for somewhere else to live. She would start to look for that flat which she had told her mother she would be seeking. She'd need an address to give Mother and Maxine anyway. And, while she had no notion as to how long Trent thought he might wait, it wouldn't be a bad idea to find some alternative accommodation sooner rather than later. Somehow, in her mind she had already left home. She felt that she would not want to return when the time came to leave Trent.

When Alethea got to her office it was all fixed in her head. Perhaps Trent had been right when he had pleasantly documented how she'd intended looking for somewhere else to live, so what was wrong with his place?

Nothing at all. The only thing he didn't know was that, though move in with him she would, there was absolutely no chance that she might one night take a moonlight saunter from her bedroom to his. She found she was smiling—he didn't deserve any better.

'Morning, Alethea, you look cheerful,' Carol greeted her.

'Morning, Carol,' she answered, and, utterly useless at subterfuge, she owned, 'I've made the momentous decision to leave home.' The topic was still much to the forefront of her mind.

'You'll enjoy it once you get used to it,' Carol assured her. 'Have you found somewhere?'

Wild horses would not have her telling anybody that she had. She only hoped Trent would be as discreet; she'd just die if Mr Chapman or anyone else at Gale Drilling found out. 'Not yet. I thought I'd start looking today.'

'Check with our accommodation section,' Carol suggested. 'They might be able to help.'

'Now why didn't I think of that?' Alethea laughed.

'Probably because it's only recently been set up,' Carol answered. And, the day pleasantly begun, they got down to work.

When Carol went in to see Mr Chapman, Alethea reached for the phone—and then hesitated. Her decision was made, and the sooner she told Trent about it, the sooner he would issue the instruction to call off the prosecution against Keith Lawrence. Yet it embarrassed her that Trent might think any early call meant that she couldn't wait to move in with him.

Against that, though, she wanted this done and out of the way. And if Trent's day went at all along the lines of Mr Chapman's, then his appointments could start first thing and he could be out of his office for the rest of the day. Alethea hesitated no more; she dialled.

Her call was taken by Dianne Tustin, and Alethea grew tense as she waited for Trent's PA either to fob her off or inform her that he wasn't in his office. But, 'I'm putting you through.' The PA's warm tones drifted down the wire, and Alethea didn't know how she felt then. Had Trent told his PA to put Alethea Pemberton through if she rang—and why? Or had he merely instructed that he wanted to speak to her if she called?

'Alethea—how are you?'

She opened her mouth; no sound came. She tried again. 'When?' she asked, and waited, and started to panic in the lengthy pause that followed: perhaps he had changed his mind? Oh, grief, for Maxine's sake, she didn't want that either.

Conversely, again she didn't know at all how she felt when at last the long pause ended and Trent suggested, 'Today?' He wanted her to move in with him *today*!

'*No!*' she said quickly, sharply. Oh, Heavens, get yourself together, woman, he'll be telling you to forget it in a minute. 'T-tomorrow,' she stammered hurriedly. 'Can we make it tomorrow?'

'As you wish,' Trent answered easily, calm where she was flustered. 'I'll come over and help you with your belongings if...'

Was he *mad*? 'No, no, that's all right.' She rushed to answer him, and felt tense again and all stewed up inside at the second pause that followed.

'You haven't told your family of your decision to move in with me?' Trent asked after some moments of silence. Had a three-legged horse won the Derby? The fact that she was moving in with him was something she wanted to keep a dark secret from *everyone*, and especially from her family. 'Would you like me to come and tell your mother...?'

Hell's bells! Alethea wondered if he was deliberately trying to give her heart failure! So much for her accusing him of being frightened of her mother! The man was terrified of no one!

'That won't be necessary,' Alethea informed him hastily. 'I mentioned to my mother at the weekend that I was going to look for somewhere. It isn't important for anyone to know exactly where,' she stated, hoping he would take the hint. 'I'll need this evening to collect my things together,' she rushed on—then, slowing down, she asked, 'If I could come to you tomorrow after work?'

'Your room will be ready for you,' Trent replied easily, and Alethea suddenly started to feel a great deal better. Given that he was a monster to suggest what he had, she quite liked him again after that comforting confirmation that she was to have her own room.

'Er—my brother-in-law?' she questioned, and found that she didn't need to add any more.

'Consider it done,' Trent said briefly, and the line went dead.

Alethea slowly put down her phone receiver. The deed was done; there was no going back now. Clearly Trent trusted her word that she would move in with him and would now be giving orders that the prosecution of Keith Lawrence be stopped. She swallowed; she only hoped she could believe in Trent's word that he would wait.

Strangely she was able to tackle her work with enthusiasm once that phone call had been made. It was mid-afternoon before she remembered Carol's suggestion that she check with the accommodation section in her efforts to find somewhere else to live.

'I'll see what I can do for you,' was the best an eager young man in the accommodation section could come up with when she had slipped out of her office and gone to that department. 'Is it urgent?'

Was it? She didn't know. 'Fairly urgent,' she smiled and, at his suggestion, gave him a list of her minimum requirements and returned to her desk. 'Fairly urgent' about covered it, she mused. Trent didn't look long on patience. Perhaps, in next to no time, he'd be telling her, It's been nice knowing you.

She left her office on time that night and drove home. Now for the sticky part. She let herself into the house and navigated a small tricycle that had been left in the already overcrowded hall. She looked on the bright side: it would be a treat to be bruise-free.

'How's everybody?' she asked, going into the sitting room.

'We've had a lovely day,' Maxine smiled, and Alethea was struck by how much better her sister was looking already.

'We went for a picnic,' Georgia put in.

'And played house in...' Sadie suddenly seemed to remember, and added quickly, 'We tidied up after...'

'It doesn't matter,' Alethea said lightly, realising that Sadie and Georgia had been playing house in her room. She had been aware that she was going to have to say something within the next few hours about her proposed departure tomorrow, and had intended to have a few words in private with her mother about it. But suddenly the opportunity was there and, taking into account that privacy seemed a thing of the past since little feet had moved in, Alethea took the plunge. 'Actually, if it's all right with Nanna and Mummy, one of you can have my room from tomorrow.' Taking her glance away from a suddenly energetic and excited Sadie, Alethea looked over to her parent. 'I've been able to find a place nearer to my job.' True. 'I'm moving in tomorrow.'

Cat amongst the pigeons didn't cover it! Though with Sadie going into ecstasies about having her own room at last, and Georgia throwing a tantrum as she put in a late bid, Eleanor Pemberton's icy displeasure did not

have the full impact on Alethea that it might
have had otherwise.

'Why don't you go upstairs and make a
start on your packing?'

Maxine interrupted her mother, who had
begun her castigation: 'Ungrateful. After all
I've done for you...'

Alethea shot her sister a grateful look.
'That might be an idea,' she murmured.

'I'll come and help,' Sadie volunteered.

'And me.'

With the help of Sadie and Georgia her
packing took twice as long, but the two
children were friends once more when Maxine
arrived to get them ready for bed.

Alethea was making tea and toast the next
morning when Maxine came down to the
kitchen to see her. 'Have you got your for-
warding address?' she asked.

'I'll let you have it later,' Alethea answered,
hoping Maxine would think she couldn't remember it off hand. 'You can always reach
me at the office if you need to. Though I'll
be back to see you all, naturally.'

'Don't be in too much of a hurry,' Maxine
advised. 'You should have moved out years
ago,' she added, as Alethea stared at her in

surprise. 'Spread your wings—live a little,' she urged, and added, laughing, 'And for Heaven's sake forget every word of "good advice" your mother ever gave you.'

Alethea had to laugh too. 'Were you always this wicked?' she asked.

'Of course. You and me—we both take after Father.'

'Do we?'

'Hell—love her though I do, and grateful though I am that she took me and the girls in—I'd cut my throat if I thought I took after Mother,' Maxine stated.

'You're incorrigible!' Alethea exclaimed, but added gently, 'You're also beginning to feel better, aren't you?'

Maxine nodded. 'It was hard, the initial break from Keith. But, thanks to you and your help in putting in a good word with his employer, I can stop worrying and start planning. I've had one chance, but there'll be other chances,' she said, sounding more positive than she had in a long while. 'But right now it's *your* chance.'

Chance? Alethea took her mother up a cup of tea. 'I'll be in touch,' she offered gently.

'Don't bother on my account,' her mother answered sourly, and there seemed nothing more for Alethea to say.

With her car boot laden with cases, she drove to her place of work with very mixed feelings. Half of her started to feel elated the further she got away from her old home—at last she had made the break! She acknowledged she had been going to leave anyway, without Trent's untimely assistance—the other half of her wondered what she was getting into.

She seemed to function on automatic pilot that day; her mind was not a hundred percent on her work. She found something else to think about when she returned from her lunch break, however, when Nick Saunders stopped by her office on the way to his.

'Ah, I'm glad I've caught you,' he smiled.

Alethea remembered he had only joined the firm on Monday. 'How are you getting on?' she asked pleasantly.

'Enjoying everything,' he answered, and added, 'I've still got five minutes before I'm due back. So, on a non-work basis, I've theatre tickets for Saturday. Would you like to come?'

Nick Saunders was a nice enough man and Alethea liked the theatre. But the opportunity as to whether or not she would have considered his invitation was lost when she all at once realised that, by moving in with Trent, the freedom she had once had to go out with whom she pleased had just been severely curtailed.

'I'm sorry,' she apologised quickly, 'I'm busy this weekend.'

'I thought you would be; it was a long shot,' he said good-humouredly. 'I can see I shall have to ask a fortnight in advance.'

Nick Saunders went from her mind soon after he had disappeared back to his own office. But not the irksome fact he had left behind. Maxine had spoken of this being her chance; presumably she meant the chance to be free, to date or not, to make decisions without having to risk anyone's disapproval.

But what chance of freedom now? Somehow she didn't think it was part and parcel of Trent's idea that, while he was waiting the long wait for her to present herself in his room, other men should come ringing his doorbell calling for her.

Suddenly she frowned. What about him? Trent was a sophisticated, virile man. Whose doorbell would he be ringing while he waited? Oddly, she discovered that she did not care for the notion that Trent might feel free to date where he chose.

She pushed thoughts of him out of her mind, deciding that it was only natural, surely, that she should not care for him spending any nights out on the tiles while she lived with him—it was only common decency.

When five o'clock came around, Alethea admitted to a great reluctance to drive to Trent's home. It was too late now to start to have second thoughts about what she was doing, too late, at this stage, to be nervous.

'There's nothing more here that won't wait until morning,' Carol observed, picking up her bag. Bang went her excuse to work late.

She went out of the building with Carol, but when they parted Alethea still wasn't ready to drive to Trent's home. A delaying tactic it might be, but she had started to convince herself that he was bound to work late.

Not fancying sitting outside his address waiting for him to come home, Alethea went and had something to eat—and made it last until seven.

At half past seven, however, her nerves had reached such a pitch that she was inwardly all of a tremble. Alethea reached his door. She rang the bell and, trying hard not to think about what she was doing, she waited.

She did not have to wait long. The evil moment was at hand. She heard him at the other side of the door. Then saw him. But he did not look at all pleased to see her!

And that was just what she needed. 'Did I get it wrong?' she demanded, surveying his stern expression.

'Wrong?' he clipped.

'If there's no room at the inn I can easily—' His face creased into a sudden grin at her spirit, causing her to break off.

'What, and miss the chance of a lifetime?' he countered, suddenly good-humoured as he revealed, 'I expected you before this. I have to go out.'

'Oh, I'm sorry,' she apologised at once, but began to wonder what this man was doing to her. While she experienced a feeling of great relief that she didn't have to spend her evening with him, she also felt a touch peeved that on this, her first evening in his home, he had to go out. She hoped his lady had a flat doorbell battery, whoever she was.

'Not to worry,' Trent answered casually. And, whether he was late for his 'appointment' or not, he enquired practically, 'You do have luggage?'

'In the boot.'

With Trent doing the lion's share of the carrying, they emptied her car. 'We might as well take your cases straight up,' he stated, and, with him leading the way, Alethea nervously followed up the stairs.

There were one or two very nice pictures on the walls, she noticed as they went up to the next landing. But just then looking at pictures was not her first priority.

Trent took her along the landing and opened the door of a room a couple of doors down. Going in, he deposited the two cases he was carrying down onto the lushly piled cream carpet.

Her nerves were showing, she knew that they were, as she put down the smaller case she was carrying, her glance skimming over the rest of the exquisite furniture and furnishings and fixing on the double bed.

'D-did you make it? The b-bed, I mean?' she asked jerkily, realising that her attempt at casual conversation was a disaster.

'Mrs Wheeler comes in Mondays, Wednesdays and Fridays,' Trent answered, and then, giving her a sharp, all-assessing look, suggested, 'Let me show you the rest of the house,' and led the way from her room.

Strangely, when she thought he would have made a point of showing her in which room he slept, he did nothing of the kind. Instead, leaving the bedroom area, he showed her over the rest of the house.

'Mrs Wheeler has left a casserole to be heated up, and there's salad in the fridge,' he informed her when they ended up in the kitchen. It seemed churlish to mention that she had already eaten. 'I usually start my day early, so help yourself to anything you fancy for breakfast.' She wasn't expected to get up and get him his, then!

While awarding him a few merit points on that account, Alethea found herself again in that topsy-turvy world which she had become familiar with since knowing Trent. For, while she was starting to feel relieved that, by the sound of it, she would be fast asleep when he returned home, and that she would not see him in the morning either, at the same time she experienced a most peculiar irritated sensation; it seemed a flat doorbell battery would be no deterrent to his nocturnal activities.

'Here's a key to the front door,' Trent stated matter-of-factly, taking a key from his pocket and handing it to her. And, checking his watch, he added, 'I've just time to show you where to garage your car, then I must be off.'

Alethea went back upstairs after he had gone. It was strange being on her own as she started to unpack her belongings. She was in the act of taking some of her toiletries into the adjoining bathroom when she suddenly realised exactly why. There was peace and quiet!

Probably because she was minus her two 'helpers', it took her much less time to empty her cases than it had taken to fill them. Once done, though, and everything neat and tidy, she went downstairs to the kitchen and made herself a coffee. While trying to absorb the feel of Trent's elegant home, she all at once found that she was quite enjoying the silence.

That would never do, she realised, and swiftly washed and dried her cup and saucer, tidied the already tidy kitchen, and returned upstairs to bed.

Her bed was comfortable, but she had not expected to sleep and did not. It was bothersome lying there awake in the darkened room. Alethea knew that she was growing tense again as she waited for Trent to come home.

She tried to tell herself that she had nothing to worry about. For goodness' sake, Trent had more about him than to come into her room the minute he came home and set about assuaging the desire he'd intimated he had for her.

Intimated! Grief, he had more than intimated. Why did she think he wanted her there in his home? And what did she know of him anyway? What did she know of any man, or how to handle the circumstance she was in?

Alethea was trying desperately to be calm, when she heard the outer door quietly open and close. Trent was home! She listened, her ears attuned for every sound. She heard faint footsteps that indicated he had made it to the top of the landing, then her straining ears picked up the sound of him coming nearer.

His footsteps would stop when they reached his door, she knew. But—they didn't! Her heart seemed to stop altogether when he came to her door and halted. Her nerves were at screaming-pitch when she heard the handle being turned! She was staring at the door when it opened and a shaft of light silhouetted Trent from behind. Her heart went instantly from stop to rapid thunder when she saw his tall outline standing there. Swiftly she closed her eyes, feigning sleep.

Then, however, while her heart was thudding so loudly she thought Trent must hear it, she heard her door quietly being closed again. Her eyes shot wide—she was alone!

Alethea lay in tense silence for another ten minutes before she dared allow herself to relax. She jumped nervously at the first sound of movement in the next-door room. Then she heard other faint muffled noises. Then silence.

As Alethea started to unwind she knew that she had been right in her first thoughts about Trent. True, he had come into her room, but it was also true that Trent had much more about him than to set about slaking any desire he felt for her the moment he came home.

She closed her eyes—and was astonished to find that when she opened them again, it was morning! Amazed that she had slept soundly and dreamlessly and that, after her initial scare, she had not continued to lie there fearing that Trent might return, Alethea could hardly believe she'd had such a good night's rest. She'd never slept as well as that in her old home!

A sound of the outer door closing jerked her into an awareness that today was a working day and that Trent had already left to start his. She checked the digital clock radio by the side of the bed. Heavens! It wasn't seven o'clock yet!

'Work!' she said determinedly, but, since living closer to her job meant she didn't have to leave as early as before, she decided she would have a cup of tea first and *then* go and get showered and ready.

Donning her blue fluffy dressing gown and blue slippers, Alethea left her room and went down the stairs. She had got no further than the hall, though, when the sound of a key in the door-lock caused her to freeze.

Like someone hypnotised, she stared at the door as Trent, business-suited and briefcase in hand, came in. 'I thought you'd gone!' she exclaimed.

She stared up at him from wide violet eyes. He was close, unnerving—and she felt foolish. 'I had,' he answered, his dark eyes fixed on her.

Alethea felt too mesmerised to move. 'Did you forget something?' she asked. She had meant to say it lightly, but her voice came out sounding husky.

Trent looked at her a few moments more, but as she started to become exceedingly conscious of her tousled hair and the fact that she wasn't wearing a scrap of make-up, he smiled.

It was a gentle smile. 'I did,' he replied, and, as if charmed by what he saw, he stared down at her a moment longer. Then, before she could break out of her trance, he had placed his briefcase on the hall table and caught a quiet hold of her. His head came nearer and she still couldn't move. 'You look all warm and cuddlesome,' he murmured, and, his arms coming about her, Alethea felt his mouth over hers.

She didn't think she kissed him back, but was so confused again that she couldn't be sure. She felt oddly safe in his arms, secure, and her heart was pounding. 'You're going to be late for work,' she found her husky voice to inform him. Grief, it still wasn't seven in the morning yet, and he was the boss, so what did it matter that he might be a little adrift on time? Feeling foolish again, she moved to be free of his arms.

Trent let her go immediately. 'Oh—we can't have that,' he teased—and went.

Having earlier set her course kitchenwards, it was in the kitchen Alethea eventually found herself. She sank down onto a chair, realising that instinct must have guided her in that direction because her thoughts were fully taken up elsewhere.

Last night she had been scared and fearful. But, just now, Trent had kissed her and she hadn't felt in the least afraid. Indeed, far from feeling scared and fearful, his kiss, astoundingly, had made her feel a little exhilarated!

She stood up and shook her head slowly once, from side to side, as if to deny it. Then, forgetting every bit about that cup of tea, she said out loud, 'Tosh!' Determining to find a place of her own soonest, she went upstairs to get ready to go to work.

CHAPTER SIX

ONE of the first things Alethea did when she got to her office was to ring through to the accommodation section and ask them to amend her file from 'fairly urgent' to just plain 'urgent'. Then work took over.

She had lunch out, worked late, and went home to the house she temporarily shared with Trent—to find that he was working even later. Either that, or he had an early 'appointment' with someone. Huh! As if she cared!

She went upstairs to change. He could have phoned to say he'd be late. Alethea shrugged out of her office suit and put on jeans and a shirt, and went down the stairs again, admitting to herself yet again that she felt herself to be a mass of contradictions.

Where would he phone, for goodness' sake? Her office? She'd love that, wouldn't she? She'd just about die of embarrassment if Carol took a call from Trent's PA and then, prior to switching the call to her desk, told

143

her that Mr Trenton de Havilland was wanting to speak to her. Grief! It didn't bear thinking about.

Alethea made herself a drink and a sandwich, watched a half-hour of television, but couldn't settle. At nine o'clock she had definitely decided that Trent was off on some doorbell-ringing activity and that she didn't give tuppence about that, when she heard his key in the door.

She decided she had things to do in her room. She was on her feet ready to walk, when, briefcase in hand, Trent came into the drawing room. They both halted, and stared at each other.

He looks tired, she thought, and only then did she take into account the work hours he'd put in that day. 'Can I get you something?' she asked impulsively, not having meant to offer any such help.

After a surprised moment he found a half-smile. It was as if, accustomed to fending for himself, he was pleased that she should so offer. 'You're lovely in person as well as body,' he said. Coming closer, he added, 'And I think I'm going to enjoy living with you.'

Don't get used to it, I'm not going to be around that long! 'Have you had anything to eat?' she asked, not from impulse this time, but more so that he should know she had no wish whatsoever to discuss anything to do with his enjoyment of living with her.

'I had a sandwich at the office about an hour ago,' Trent answered. While the contradictory side of her felt uplifted at his confirmation that he had been at work the whole while, she also scoffed at her elation.

'I've things to do upstairs, so I'll say goodnight,' she informed him crisply, and was on her way past him when his hand snaked out and, catching hold of her arm, he brought her round to face him. She stared at him warily and saw that his half-smile was a thing of the past; he was not best pleased with her.

'You've no need to be nervous of me, Alethea!' he told her curtly.

Not much! Anger put her nervousness to flight. 'This from a man whose sole purpose in having me to live with him is so he can have his—his—way with me?' she charged, glad to have her spirit back.

'Only ever with your consent!' he rapped.

'You should live that long!' she fired. She wanted to hit him when he burst out laughing, as if she amused him.

She didn't wait for anything more. Pulling her arm from his hold, she marched from the room. Swine! Swine! How dared he laugh at her?

Strangely, she slept soundly again that night. And, once more, she awakened just in time to hear Trent leaving. This time he did not come back.

It had been Alethea's intention to check out apartment agencies in her lunch hour. But late that morning she had a call from the company accommodation section to say they had just taken delivery of the keys of a very nice flat; would she like to take a look at it?

'Yes, please,' she said without hesitation. At least she wouldn't be put onto the street when Trent got fed up with waiting for her consent.

She took a look at the basement flat in her lunch hour. Given that it was in an area that wasn't as plush as the location where Trent had his home, the situation was still quite good. There were iron railings curtaining off the basement from the road, and, after going down stone steps, Alethea inserted one of two keys, and quite liked the idea of having her own front door.

She went into a small hall and liked most everything else about that too. The kitchen wasn't anything to rave about, but the sitting room was large, and led out into a garden. The only thing she did not like, and which she knew she could not live with, was the colour of the bedroom walls.

If you liked dark green with splashes of red, fine. First things first; Alethea went back to Gale Drilling International and told the accommodation section that she would like to take the flat. And, having agreed to take it straight away, she went back to her office trying to calculate how many gallons of pastel-shaded paint it was going to take to cover the dark green and red walls.

She could not resist going to take another look at what was now 'her flat' on her way home. She felt good about it. It was hers. A place of her own.

Alethea was late getting back to Trent's home, but he was going to be even later. Well, bubbles to him! She was glad she had her basement flat. If nothing else, it would give her something else to think about than him.

Only then did she realise how much Trent was in her mind. But then, why wouldn't she think of him often? Who wouldn't in her situation?

She had already decided she was going to have another early night when, just after eight-thirty, Trent came home. She did not make the mistake of asking him if she could get him anything.

He asked her. 'Going to make me a cup of coffee?'

Sprained your wrist? She looked at him and surmised from the fine lines round his eyes that he must have had a wearying day. 'Love to,' she heard herself say, and took herself off to the kitchen, only to feel thoroughly exasperated when Trent followed her and stood and watched her. He could just as easily have made his own coffee!

'Aren't you going to have one too?' he asked when she took out only one cup and saucer.

Plainly he was asking her to join him. She had been going to go upstairs. Then she remembered how last night he had spotted that she was nervous of him. It then seemed a point of honour that he did not continue to think so.

'How was your day?' she asked, opening the cupboard again and getting out another cup and saucer.

'Full,' he answered.

'Is your work highly confidential?' She found she was interested in what he did.

'Some of it,' he agreed, and, even though there was a most comfortable drawing room in which to sit and drink coffee, they found themselves seated at the kitchen table with their cups in front of them. 'Some of our scientists are asked to help with projects abroad when some sort of problem crops up.' He had said that he was away a great deal too, so she rather guessed that he went to lead his team when extra expertise was called for. 'How about you?' he asked. 'How was your day?'

Her honesty was such that she wanted to tell him about the flat the accommodation section had found for her. But, somehow, she found herself holding back. 'Full,' she answered, and, having repeated his word back at him, she had to smile.

She saw his glance go to her curving mouth, and felt all over the place when, his look steady, he transferred his gaze to her eyes. 'You know,' he said quietly after some moments just looking at her, 'I find it incredible that you're sitting here like this.'

Alethea made valiant attempts to get herself together. 'That makes two of us!' she said crisply, got up and went to bed.

She did not sleep so well that night. She seemed to be in bed half a lifetime before she heard Trent coming up the stairs. She tensed, but his footsteps came no nearer than to his own bedroom door. Her confidence that he would only ever make love to her with her consent started to grow. Although she rather supposed she had believed that from the moment he had first given his word that he would wait. It was just that she'd had a big adjustment to make. It had been more easy to believe his word when she had been able to say goodnight and go to her own home. But it was unnervingly different in these initial hours in the close, intimate confines of Trent's home—the place where she temporarily lived.

She heard the faint sounds of him moving about next door. But even when those sounds had long since faded, she was still no nearer to falling asleep. She slept only fitfully and was awake early.

Having lain there awake for what seemed like hours, Alethea had suddenly had enough of bed. All was silent next door. Quietly, not wanting to disturb Trent if he was in the habit of having an extra hour in bed at the weekends, Alethea got up, donned her dressing gown and slippers, and tiptoed from her bedroom and went down the stairs.

Going into the kitchen, she set about making a pot of tea, with her thoughts anywhere but on what she was doing. She found herself reflecting on the long hours Trent put in. Not that she was concerned about him in any way; it was just that, working so hard, when did he play?

The weekend, that was when, she didn't doubt. Why, only last Saturday—was it only last Saturday?—he'd been going to have a party... Grief, she hoped he wasn't thinking of having another tonight, of having people round. She was going to make herself scarce if he was.

Alethea looked down at what she was doing, and discovered that, from force of habit, she had poured out two cups of tea. She took one with her to a kitchen chair, but before she could start sipping, she found her eyes going again and again to the other cup on the work-top, sitting there accusingly.

He worked so hard. Oh, dammit! She was on her feet, finding a tray. Why was she so mean-spirited when he worked so hard, when she had actually poured a second cup, as not to take one up to him?

All the way up the stairs Alethea fought a losing battle against doing a smart about-turn and taking the tray back down the stairs again. Outside Trent's bedroom door she engaged in another battle. She wasn't mean-spirited, she knew that she wasn't, it was just that... Oh, don't be ridiculous!

Impatience with herself won the day and, in the next moment, after a brief tap on his door, Alethea opened it and went in. It was too late then to change her mind.

A swift glance to the bed showed that Trent was awake. Indeed he was sitting up in bed and had been reading what looked like some business report or other, the pages of which he slowly lowered as, tea-tray in hand, she approached the bed.

Oh, grief, the duvet was a little way up to his ribcage. But, from the naked upper half of him, she had an idea that he hadn't anything on!

'Good morning,' she said briskly, and intended to place his cup of tea on his bedside table and get out of there quickly. 'I didn't put any sugar in,' she added in a rush.

'I'm sure it will be good for me,' he drawled, and she didn't know whether to laugh or hit him!

That confusion again! Nerves, of course, simply nerves. She found a small space on his bedside table and took the cup and saucer from the tray and placed them there. But when she went to execute a rapid turn and make a hasty exit, Trent caught a hold of her wrist. She looked down at his long, muscled but naked arm, and froze.

'Don't rush off,' he said easily, and she glanced at him again.

The outstretched movement of his arm had caused the duvet to fall down to his waist. His chest was broad, had dark hair on it, and she could see his nipples.

Oh, Lord! She swiftly raised her eyes to his face, hoping that she didn't look as pink about the cheeks as she felt. 'You need a shave,' she blurted out, needing to say something, anything.

'Shall I get out of bed and do that now?' Trent volunteered wickedly, and Alethea knew for a certain then that he was stark naked underneath that duvet! Also, he was tormenting her for the pure hell of it. But he relented and gave her wrist a small tug, which caused her to sit on his bed next to him. 'Thank you for the tea; it was a very sweet gesture,' he smiled.

She didn't know quite how she felt, sitting on his bed with barely a yard separating them. 'I—um—always took my mother a cup of tea in bed,' she managed.

'I hope you don't look on me as your mother,' Trent drawled, letting go of her wrist, and she had to laugh.

'You work so hard.' She felt she should further explain her action. 'Off at first light, returning late,' she documented.

'You've noticed?' She thought he seemed pleased. 'Do you miss me? My...'

'I hardly know you!' She let him know that straight away. Though, given that he hadn't got a stitch on under that cover—Heavens above, how had she ever got herself into this situation?—and that, although respectable, she was not dressed herself yet, she reckoned they could no longer be said to be just mere acquaintances.

'Then I suggest we remedy that without delay,' Trent answered. Her eyes flew to his in sudden panic. She wasn't sure that she hadn't jumped a few inches. But she soon discovered that she had not the smallest need to panic, that he wasn't suggesting that she join him in his bed. Even while his eyes were watchful, Trent's voice was calming as he asked, 'How about we spend the day together?'

Alethea at once started to feel less panicky. 'Oh, I'm...' She wasn't sure how she felt about spending her day with him, wasn't sure she wanted to know him any better. 'I've a lot to do today,' she excused, but found that the decision of whether or not to spend the day with him had just been taken from her.

'It will wait,' Trent stated decisively. 'I'm flying to South America early tomorrow for three weeks.'

'Some people have jam on it!' she snorted, to cover the fact that, quite unexpectedly, she didn't feel at all happy that it would be ages before she would see him again. What rot! she scolded to herself. But she discovered that she had weakened—sufficiently, anyhow, to offer, 'Well, I suppose I could put my plans on ice—if that's what you want.'

'That's what I want,' Trent agreed. 'Got a good morning kiss for me?' he teased.

'Make do with a cup of tea!' Alethea told him tartly, and saw him grin. The oddest feeling came over her that she would quite like to feel the briefest touch of his mouth over hers again, and she knew it was time to get out of there. She left him abruptly and, her own tea forgotten in the kitchen, she went to get showered, feeling a little mixed-up.

While Trent had a car that could outpace many others on the road, he drove without hurry. Sometimes they chatted, at other times they didn't. By the time they drove into Wiltshire, taking the scenic route, Alethea was feeling totally relaxed with him. She again acknowledged that she liked him, must do, or she wouldn't be here with him now.

'Have you been in touch with your family since you left?' Trent asked as they sat sipping coffee in a hotel.

'I only left last Wednesday,' she reminded him.

'Any problems?' he enquired.

'Thanks for asking,' she muttered. But he heard, and seemed amused at her hint that she'd have appreciated him putting that question to her last Wednesday.

'Bad as that, was it?'

She was about to deny it but, remembering her mother's attitude, it could not have been said to be good. '*Do* you take sugar in your tea, by the way?' she asked, and saw his mouth twitch as she swiftly changed the subject.

'As a matter of fact, no,' he answered, and she wanted to laugh—there was just something about the man.

They left the car in the hotel's car park and went for a leg-stretching walk around. Then they drove on for a while, and Trent, seeming to instinctively know a good place to stop from a bad one, pulled up at an unpretentious-looking hotel for lunch, which just happened to serve the most delicious food.

'I've just got to have another walk after that,' Alethea told him. She had a good appetite, but was lucky enough never to put on a spare pound.

'You and me, both,' Trent agreed. He looked across at her lovely face. 'May I say what a pleasure it is to be with a woman who isn't afraid to walk a yard or two.'

'Too kind, sir,' Alethea replied primly. 'And may I be permitted to say, you've been going out with the wrong type.'

Again he looked at her, seemed to enjoy looking at her, and she stared back at him, wondering just what type of woman he usually went for. By the sound of it, sophisticated types like him. The bring-the-car-round-to-the-door-James-type. Sultry, elegant, beautiful, undoubtedly.

Abruptly she stood up. 'I'll find the ladies' room and see you presently,' she managed to get out, and took herself off in haste.

In the ladies' room she ran a brush through her blonde hair and tried to come to terms with the dreadful feeling she had experienced at the table with Trent a short while back.

Several reasons presented themselves for why she had felt almost wounded, but she dismissed them.

She would have liked to blame that dreadful feeling on something she had eaten. But the roast duck with black cherry sauce had been superb. It was with a great deal of reluctance she acknowledged at last that, when thinking of the other women in Trent's life, she had been jealous.

Jealous! She had never been jealous in her life! It took some minutes before she could accept that she was jealous of the other women Trent went out with. But it was a fact.

Did that then mean that she wanted to be like them? Did she want to be sophisticated and elegant? She looked at her reflection in the cloakroom mirror. She wore a knee-length fine wool dress and, she supposed, looked smart enough. But, she hadn't reached sophistication yet, and didn't know about elegant—and you could forget all about sultry.

Honest, if nothing else, Alethea probed deeper. So, why was she jealous? If not because of his women, then perhaps because Trent went out with such women. She liked him, she faced that. But would that alone account for her jealousy?

The answer proved elusive, but then Alethea found she was wondering if Trent truly normally went out with such sophisticated types as she imagined. She realised he must when she considered his remark about a woman who wasn't afraid to walk a yard or two. So why, then, was he going out with her?

Grief, she thought a moment later, she knew why: he wanted her in his bed, and she was proving resistant to the idea. A man like Trent thrived on challenges. Oh, Heavens!

It took Alethea another five minutes before she felt ready to go and join Trent again. Not that he seemed to be fretting at her absence. He was standing in the foyer in conversation with a sombrely suited member of staff.

He spotted her straight away, though. 'All right?' he asked, coming over to her and escorting her from the hotel.

'Fine,' she answered, and realised that she was all at once feeling fine.

'Good. Let's walk,' Trent said. 'I've just been talking to the hotel manager. He said if we turn right at the end here it leads to a lane, which leads to a public right of way, at the end of which there's a bridge with a stream.'

'Sounds idyllic,' she answered, and discovered twenty minutes or so later that it was.

There was something fascinating about watching rippling water meandering on its way, Alethea decided. There was also something quite enchanting about the peace and quiet of their surroundings, in the many shades of green in the grass and leaves on the trees. There was something quite harmonious about it all.

So why did Trent have to go and spoil it by asking, 'Do you ever see your father?'

She felt a flicker of irritation. 'Not now,' she answered.

'Which means you did?'

Honestly! Watch the water! Look at the trees! 'At first,' she replied crisply, and wanted to thump Trent when he would not let the subject go. Where, she had to pause to wonder, did all her aggression come from? She was normally calm, not easily roused to anger—but this man! From almost the first he had turned her nice, calm, safe world upside-down.

Alethea concentrated hard on admiring the view, something which, not so long back, had needed no concentration at all. 'It's lovely here.' She felt tense and in the need to say something.

'Beautiful,' Trent murmured, and she just had to turn her head and take a quick look at him. He wasn't admiring the view, she saw, but her. Quickly she turned her head away. She felt strung up and all over the place. Yet Trent's voice was casual, off-hand almost, as he enquired, 'So what did you plan to do today that might have prevented you from enjoying this view?'

Alethea at once recalled how she had originally turned down his invitation because she had a lot to do that day. Perhaps it was the fact that his tone was so casual, or perhaps it was that she needed something to pin her thoughts. Whatever the case, Alethea discovered that she did not have the same reluctance to tell him about her flat that she had experienced last evening.

'I've taken a flat,' she stated. 'It needs—' She got no further.

'The devil you have!' The roar of Trent's voice, so totally unlike his previous casual tone, made her turn sharply to stare at him. 'You're living with me!' he informed her furiously.

'As if I need reminding!' In an instant she was as angry as he, the peace and quiet of the afternoon shattered as, toe-to-toe, they glared at each other. Then, suddenly, just when she was certain that some acid retort was on its way to her lips, her innate honesty came and tripped her up. Moving in with him had not been compulsory; she had done it to gain what she wanted and it was a bargain that she had agreed to. Her anger dipped. 'Don't be sniffy about it, Trent,' she said, starting to feel miserable. While she still had no intention of fulfilling her part of the bargain to the letter, she had, after all, in her mind agreed to live with him until such time as he told her to go. Trent continued to eye her with hostility. Which left her to explain, 'You know as well as I do that our—er—arrangement isn't a permanent one.'

He eyed her coldly for perhaps two seconds or more, and then enquired coolly, 'You're suggesting it will soon be over?'

At once misery vanished and she came out fighting. 'Don't get your hopes up, de

Havilland!' she flared. 'I'm no closer to getting into your bed now than I've ever been!'

What she expected him to say in reply she had no idea. What she did not expect, however, was that, she having told him what was what, he should stare at her and, as she stared back at him, that she should see his lips start to twitch. Suddenly, so did hers.

'You're the limit,' he commented and it was the most natural thing in the world that he accompanied those words with a brief kiss on her mouth.

Both pulled back. She felt no alarm and, strangely, no surprise. She looked at him, saw his gaze on her was steady, serious. His head came down once more towards her.

He put his arms around her. She liked feeling this close to him. His lips captured hers, gentle, seeking, giving and yet taking, not greedily.

She placed her hands on his waist and kissed him back when, for a third time, he kissed her. When three kisses simply begged to be four, he kissed her again and she relaxed totally, putting her arms around him.

Trent raised his head, warmth in his eyes. 'This is one hell of a way to work off lunch.'

'Perhaps we'd better walk,' she suggested.

But for long, long seconds they just stood and looked at each other, until he agreed, 'Perhaps we better had.' As they walked he kept one arm about her shoulders, almost as if it fitted, as if that was where it belonged. Alethea did not object. Away from his house, out here in this splendid countryside, she felt in no way threatened.

They spent what was left of the afternoon walking, talking and driving and in a fine kind of harmony. They returned to London in the early evening.

'You'll have to pack for your trip, I expect,' she realised as they entered his drawing room.

'It won't take long,' he replied. 'Hungry?'

'You did all the driving; I'll get us something to eat,' she offered. They didn't need another mammoth meal that day. 'Poached eggs all right?'

'So tell me about this flat you've had the nerve to take,' he invited when they were sitting down in the kitchen to supper.

Alethea darted a quick look at him, but saw his question was asked good-humouredly.

'It's a basement flat, and I'll need to decorate... That's what I intended to do today, go and decide how much exactly has to be done and how much emulsion or wallpaper I'll need—whichever I decide on.'

'You're going to decorate it yourself?'

'I thought I'd try.'

'Are you any good at paper-hanging?' he asked, seeming interested.

She shook her head. 'I've never done any before, which is why I shall probably use emulsion,' she grinned. 'Though, come to think of it, I've never emulsioned a wall before either.'

'I'll...' he began, and seemed to change his mind about what he intended to say. 'I'm sure you'll do a splendid job,' he stated encouragingly.

Their acquaintance—Alethea didn't think it could be called a relationship—seemed to have moved into a different sort of sphere, she rather felt. She supposed having spent the day with each other, having exchanged several kisses—more in friendship than as lovers—had a lot to do with it. But, even so, she was sipping the last of her coffee when she suddenly began to get the notion that Trent was only waiting for her to say goodnight so he could go and get on with his packing.

She carried the dishes to the sink and began to wash them. When Trent came over and, picking up a cloth, began to dry the dishes, she grew more certain that he was now in a hurry to make a start on his packing.

Alethea checked that everything was tidy and, remembering she had left her shoulder bag in the drawing room, she went to retrieve it.

'Nightcap?' Trent enquired, following her in.

'I think I'll go to bed,' she refused in a friendly fashion.

'Sure?'

He was standing quite close. 'Positive,' she smiled, and found she was telling him honestly, 'I enjoyed today. Thank you.'

Trent smiled too, and took two steps that brought him within touching distance. 'I enjoyed it too,' he stated softly, his eyes fixed on hers.

Feeling unable to move, Alethea stared up at him. She still hadn't moved when he stretched forward, caught hold of her by her upper arms, and placed his superb warm mouth against her own.

She had closed her eyes, but she quickly opened them when he broke his kiss and pulled back from her, before abruptly walking away. 'Goodnight, Alethea,' he said evenly. Making for the drinks table, he made no move to detain her.

Clearly kissing her had not deprived him of his fancy for a nightcap! Feeling most peculiarly disgruntled—grief, what was she waiting for, to be kissed again?—she went swiftly to bed.

But she couldn't get off to sleep. Much later she heard Trent coming up the stairs. Then, as on previous nights, she heard him moving about in his room. She knew that he was packing and felt, ridiculously, that she would like to go and help him.

I must be going soft in the head, she decided. Trent, by the sound of it, was always going away and would therefore be highly efficient at packing.

She was all confused again by the time sleep claimed her. Most oddly, she had realised that it was comforting hearing Trent moving about next door. Also, she dearly wished she had asked him what time he was leaving in the morning. Insanely she felt that she would like to get up to see him off. Well, why shouldn't she? He was going to be away for three weeks, he'd said. Her thoughts were starting to grow more confused, the drowsier she got. She wouldn't see him now for three whole weeks! She fell asleep arguing with herself: as if it mattered that she wouldn't see him again before he went!

But she did see Trent again before he left, however. She opened her eyes and saw him placing a cup of tea down on her bedside table.

'Didn't see why early-morning tea-delivery should be your sole prerogative,' he said, on seeing her waking.

She struggled to sit up, sleepy still, but glad to see him, she realised. 'Are you going now?' she asked.

'Very shortly,' he replied, and, coming to sit on the side of her bed, he asked, 'Going to be good while I'm away?'

'You think I should break a habit of a lifetime?' she asked impishly.

His mouth tweaked at the corners. 'You will one day,' he informed her solemnly. But that

half-smile was back again when he added ro-
guishly, 'And I intend to be there.'

She laughed. She liked him. 'Don't hold
your breath,' she advised, and was soundly
kissed for her trouble.

But when Trent pulled back neither of them
was laughing. She stared at him unblinking—
she didn't want him to go! Trent stared back
and for ageless moments they just looked at
each other. Then, abruptly, he switched his
gaze from her face and his glance happened
to light on where the loose-fitting strap of her
nightdress had fallen down, way down.

Alethea followed his eyes, her breath
catching as she saw that most of her left breast
was exposed. She went to hurriedly cover
herself up. 'Don't!' Trent commanded.
'You're beautiful,' he breathed, and with a
groan, as if he was fast going out of control,
he reached for her and took her in his arms.

Unresisting, and maybe feeling a little be-
wildered, Alethea clung onto him. Then his
mouth claimed hers and, though he had kissed
her before, this time it was different.

Alethea came fully awake as the pressure
of his arms around her increased. She felt his
mouth against her own, mobile, parting her

lips with his. She was not sure if he breathed her name against her mouth. All she did know was that she had no mind to try and push him away.

Indeed, when Trent, still holding her firmly in one arm, began to caress her naked left shoulder with his other hand, far from pushing him away, Alethea nestled closer to him. When that caressing hand moved down to capture the firm globe of her uncovered breast, Alethea swallowed hard.

'Oh, my dear,' he breathed against her mouth, and kissed her, caressed her, awakening such feelings in her that she did not know where she was.

Then at last, as if compelled, Trent pulled back. His eyes searched her face, before once more, as if drawn, his glance went down to where her left breast was now fully exposed.

Her breath sucked in, but as she went to swiftly cover herself Trent's hand on her wrist prevented her. 'I won't hurt you,' he soothed quietly, and bent his head to her uncovered breast and kissed the hardened peak, then took it into his mouth, awakening in her a desire such as she had never known.

Which made it a mystery to her that she called out, 'Stop!' when what she wanted was for him to never stop.

With a deep sound of anguish, he did stop. He even righted the strap of her nightdress back on her shoulder, though he seemed to be having a devil of a time with his self-control. Letting go of her, he asked, 'You're something of a spoilsport, Alethea Pemberton—do you know that?'

Dear Heaven, she wanted him to kiss her again. 'I know it,' she managed huskily.

'Do you also know that you're driving me half-demented?'

Didn't he know what he was doing to her? 'I bet you say that to all the girls,' she said, desperately searching for something to put her back together again.

Trent looked at her long and hard, as if he might store up the memory of how she looked—all tousled hair and pinkened cheeks. Then he growled, 'I've a plane to catch!'— and was gone.

CHAPTER SEVEN

ALETHEA did not go back to sleep after Trent had left. How could she? He had awakened emotions in her at which she had never guessed. She had thought she had been kissed before, but she hadn't. Not like that. No man had ever stirred her in the way that Trent had.

She drank the tea he had brought her and mused what a lovely gesture that was on his part. Then she swiftly got out of bed and got showered and dressed, while all the time she strove to get her head back together.

She spent the morning in such a mental quagmire that she achieved little. Had that been her in Trent's arms—clinging, wanting more? Had she dreamed the whole of it?

It all seemed so crazy, though she had to admit that since first she had met him her ability to think straight had taken a dramatic downward turn. She felt pulled all ways. She hadn't wanted to come and live with him and should be hating him because he had forced her to do so.

But she didn't hate him and, if this morning's performance was anything to go by, it seemed she was growing more and more attracted to him. Oh, Heavens! No wonder she was confused.

Fully awake, and in the cold light of day, Alethea was able to re-endorse the fact that she still had not the slightest intention of getting into bed with Trent. Only now she quite urgently wished that, instead of waiting for Trent to get fed up with waiting for that event, they had agreed a time limit.

By the time the afternoon came around, it seemed to her that she had done nothing but think of Trent ever since she had opened her eyes that morning. While she did not discount that Trent and his kisses and caresses had disturbed her mightily, she decided that the fact that all her thoughts seemed centred around him must be because, this not being a working day, she had nothing to do.

Nothing to do! Ye gods, she'd got a flat that needed decorating and furnishing. Furnishing? Alethea pulled herself together once more, thought of the furniture she'd always been tripping over in her old home, and went and dialled her mother's number. Maxine answered.

'How's life living on your own?' she asked, still sounding so much brighter that Alethea had to be glad she had done what she'd done. No need to tell Maxine that she wasn't living on her own.

'Different, but I like it,' she answered.

'Good! Though I was sure you would. Where is it, by the way?'

This time Alethea had an address to give. She gave her sister the address of the basement flat, adding, 'You must come and see it when I've got it decorated and the way I want it.'

'All of us? You'll be sorry! What's your phone number?'

'I—er—can't remember,' Alethea excused, which was true. 'It's not on the handset,' she said, which was an invention. 'Actually,' she went on quickly, 'I'm on the cadge. Is Mother there?'

'She's taken Sadie and Georgia out for a walk.'

'Not Polly?'

'Would you?' Maxine asked drily, and
Alethea laughed. 'She's sleeping,' Maxine
went on to explain. 'She's played hell all
morning and is now exhausted. What are you
on the cadge for?'

'Loan, actually. I wondered if I could
borrow some of my old bedroom furniture.
Only temporarily until I can—'

'Borrow some of mine—you'd be doing us
all a favour,' Maxine cut in quickly. 'How
about your sitting room?'

Alethea put down the phone with the
problem of equipping her flat easily solved.
She had told Maxine she would arrange the
furniture's collection. Her sister was keen she
should take the chest that presently resided in
the hall. Trent had cracked his shin on that
chest, Alethea remembered—and Trent was
back in her head again.

Alethea was glad to see Monday come
around. She felt a most restless need to keep
busy. Which was no problem until she left her
office. Somehow, when she had never had a
problem in filling her evenings before, the
evening seemed to stretch before her emptily
and endlessly.

For goodness' sake, what's wrong with you? She gave herself a pep talk, and went straight from her office to her basement flat. Yes, most definitely the bedroom was going to have to be decorated before she could move in any furniture.

Alethea made a stab of calculating how many decorating materials she would need, and went back to the house she shared with Trent. Only he wasn't there, and it wasn't the same. She wasn't hungry and she was going to bed. She planned a busy day tomorrow.

Perversely she decided to make herself a warm drink first, and was in the kitchen when the telephone rang. Oh, heck! She decided against answering it. She had no idea if Trent had told anyone that he had someone living with him. But in any case she wasn't about to tell anyone who she was.

But the phone persisted in ringing, so whoever wanted Trent wasn't going to give up in a hurry. Well, it couldn't be anyone from his office because they'd know that he was out of the country. And he would certainly have told anyone close to him that he'd be away for three weeks—his parents or some close woman-friend.

Oh, dammit, that last thought somehow made her feel impatient. Before she knew it she had taken the receiver of the kitchen wall-phone in her hand and said, 'Hello.'

'Were you in the bath?' asked the voice she would know anywhere.

'Where are you?' she said crazily, her heart lifting; he must be back in England.

'Rio,' he answered, and she felt empty again; he was in Brazil. 'I thought you must be out?'

'I didn't know whether to answer the phone or not,' she quickly explained. 'I—um—didn't know if you'd told anyone that you had someone living with you.'

'My home is your home, Alethea,' he answered, which told her precisely nothing.

'Yes, well.' Her heartbeat steadied a little, and she was able to reason that he hadn't telephoned all the way from Brazil for idle chit-chat. 'What can I do for you?' she asked, picking up the pencil next to the phone notepad.

'Oh, Alethea,' Trent answered, and there was such a welter of wickedness in his voice that she realised she had left herself wide open to some remark that might make the satellite connection a little wobbly.

She coughed over a laugh, and suddenly felt happier than she had all day. 'Are you trying to corrupt me?'

'That would be impossible.'

'But you're still going to do your best?'

'Trust me,' he answered, and sounded so serious she didn't know quite what to make of his remark.

'You don't ask for much!' she retorted, 'trust' being a sore subject. 'Did you ring for anything special?' she asked.

'I need a reason to call my own number?' he returned.

He sounded indulgent, and she smiled. 'I'll say goodnight, then.'

'Keep safe,' he answered, and was gone.

Alethea slept dreamlessly and went to her office the next morning full of enthusiasm. She took time out to ring a furniture remover—and discovered that the firm was booked up weeks in advance.

'It's not a full load,' she thought to mention, and discovered the removers had a smaller van which, since the pick-up and delivery was wanted as soon as possible, they could arrange for a week on Friday afternoon.

She did not hesitate to accept and, although with Trent away for three weeks there was no particular hurry, Alethea felt that arranging furniture in her flat would nicely fill up another weekend while Trent was away.

That was when she caught herself up short. Good Heavens, when had she ever needed to plan filling up her weekends?

During her lunch hour she purchased paint brushes, a roller and emulsion paint and loaded them into the boot of her car. It was about four that afternoon, however, when her enthusiasm for flat-decorating started to wane.

To start with she'd had every intention of going to the flat straight from work that evening, and even had a change of clothes ready on the back seat of her car. But at five o'clock she decided that there was no desperate hurry to start the painting. There was over a week to go before the furniture would arrive.

Alethea left her office promptly and drove to Trent's home. She made herself a snack and rang her mother. 'Did Maxine tell you she'd agreed to let me borrow some of her furniture?' she asked.

'It will be cheaper than putting it into storage,' her mother answered sourly, giving Alethea the impression that she was having second thoughts about cramming her house full with Maxine's furniture.

'How are you?' she asked, hoping her mother might have thawed a little by now.

'Perfectly well,' Eleanor Pemberton answered coolly.

Alethea told her about the furniture remover, and arranged to visit her family home the following Saturday to find out what pieces besides that chest she might borrow. She rang off to spend the rest of the evening eyeing a silent phone. Would Trent ring tonight as he had last night?

Don't be idiotic—why would he? Nevertheless Alethea found she was having a hard time concentrating on the book she was trying to read; the same time as Trent had phoned last night was getting near.

Grief! Anyone would think she was hoping he would ring! Anyone would think she hadn't gone to the flat because she wanted to be around, should he ring early! What utter twaddle!

Trent did not telephone that night and Alethea took herself off to bed in a very mixed frame of mind. That annoyed her. Even when the wretched man wasn't around, he still had the power to confuse her.

Alethea went to her flat from her office the next evening. She hoped Trent did ring, because she wasn't waiting in for his call. She unloaded the paint and decorating materials from her car, and got busy straight away.

She enjoyed the physical labour of rubbing down walls and woodwork, though it was quite hard going. For hour after hour she laboured, determined not to think about one T. de Havilland Esquire.

Time was going on. By the time she had completed her sandpapering, she could not resist trying out the new shade. That was when she realised that getting an even covering was not as easy as it looked. She decided that she'd had enough for one day. What she needed was a shower, something to eat and bed, in that order.

She drove to Trent's home well pleased with her evening's work. She was showered, in her dressing gown, and in the kitchen making herself a sandwich when the phone rang.

She jumped, startled. It wouldn't be him! Her heart set up a busy clamour. He might ring off. She picked the phone up in something of a hurry. 'Hello!' she said breathlessly.

'Where have *you* been?' Trent demanded angrily, his tone such that any pleasantness of feeling towards him was sent flying.

Who on earth did he think he was with his demanding questions? Alethea wished she had never picked up the perishing phone! 'Still in Rio?' she enquired. Nobody spoke to her like that, ever!

'I rang earlier.'

'I was out!'

'I know *that*! Where were you?'

'Since you ask so charmingly, I've been round at my flat making a start on the decorating,' she offered, and soon realised that he didn't care very much for her sarcasm when a kind of furious roar hit her ears.

'Can't wait to leave, can you?' he snarled.

'Just say when!' she erupted.

'And what about our little arrangement?' he barked.

Little! 'Did I say I was going to break it?'

'It never crossed your mind!' he tossed in sceptically. Ever the one to give orders, he demanded, 'You'd better give me the phone number of your flat!'

Oh, no! 'I don't know it,' she said sweetly. As far as she was concerned, their conversation was over. 'Keep safe,' she added prettily, and slammed down the phone.

Keep safe! She hoped he got foot-rot. Toad! Evil swine! She didn't want her sandwich. She took herself off to bed, hating him with all her might. She might not come home at all tomorrow night—see how he liked that!

Who the Dickens did he think he was? Just because he was out of the country, he thought she should sit by the phone every night on the off-chance that he might call. Well, he could go and take a running jump! She might have agreed to their unwholesome bargain, but that didn't mean she had to stick it out meekly while she waited for him to get fed up with waiting.

She packed some sandwiches to take with her to the flat on Thursday, and drove to work. Trent was still on her mind, though, she reasoned, you could hardly have some brute snapping and snarling at you over the phone the way he had and not think about him.

At her office she concentrated on her work. In her lunch hour she went out and purchased a few kitchen utensils. She returned to find Nick Saunders about to go into her office.

'Ah, I've been looking for you!' he beamed.

'You've found me,' Alethea smiled.

'I wondered how you felt about dinner with me tomorrow?' Nick enquired.

She quite liked him, though she didn't regret having to turn him down. 'Sorry, I've plans,' she smiled.

'Which obviously don't include me,' he replied, and managed to look so dramatically downcast that she just had to laugh.

'Not unless you're any good with a paint-brush,' she commented, and went to go past him and into her office when he delayed her again.

'You're decorating?' he questioned.

Alethea nodded. 'I've just taken a flat and can't live with the walls the colour they are,' she answered. There was no reason why she shouldn't be friendly with him as far as she could see. It made for a good working at-mosphere if one spared a moment to pass a pleasant few words with a colleague.

But she was momentarily thrown when Nick Saunders' face creased into a wide grin and he said, 'Believe it or not I've just fin-ished doing out my place. I'm absolutely bril-liant at it.'

'I don't believe it,' she said lightly, and again went to go past him.

'Try me,' he suggested. 'Where is your flat?'

'I...' She hesitated. She was determined not to rush back to Trent's home tonight. Would she be so strong tomorrow. Strong? Why did she have to be strong? This was ridiculous!

'Perhaps I could do with a bit of expert advice,' she acknowledged.

'I'm your man.' Nick smiled willingly.

It was very true, Alethea found when that night she again applied the paint roller to the walls, she did need some expert advice. Were it not for the fact that she had arranged for Nick Saunders to come round tomorrow night, tomorrow morning might well have seen her looking in the yellow pages for a painter and decorator.

She went home to Trent's house feeling tired and dispirited, and wishing that he would phone. But he wouldn't. Not after last night's call. In any event, he might have designs on her but she wouldn't put it past him to be busy 'designing' away in Brazil with some Rio lovely. Damn him! She was glad she had given Nick Saunders the address of the flat. Glad he was coming round tomorrow. They might only be going to do some decorating, but at least he'd be someone to talk to!

She had never felt lonely before. She did not like the feeling. It upset her sleep pattern. It put her off her food. In fact, it upset her totally. She didn't know quite why she felt lonely, she just knew that there was a sort of aching emptiness inside her. Most odd.

Nick Saunders arrived at the basement door of her flat promptly at seven-thirty the next evening. He was dressed in paint-spattered trousers and similarly bespattered shirt. Clearly he was ready for work.

She might not be any good at decorating, but she made a very fine labourer, Alethea decided as, in between holding this, wiping that, she made yet more coffee and plied Nick with sandwiches she had bought at lunchtime.

Compared to her, Nick, as he'd said, was absolutely brilliant at decorating. Time was getting on when he declared that that was as much as he could do for the evening but that the walls and ceiling would need another covering. 'I'll come round tomorrow,' he volunteered, and Alethea started to feel a trifle awkward.

Wishing she had employed a decorator after all—Nick would be extremely offended if she offered to pay him—she said quickly, 'I—er—won't be here tomorrow. I'm sorting out furniture to bring from my mother's.' She felt in all friendliness that she should explain.

'Oh, I hadn't realised you were still living at home.' Nick smiled easily. The words to tell him differently just wouldn't come. 'Though it's obvious that without furniture you haven't moved in here yet. Fancy going out for a meal tomorrow evening?' he was quick to ask.

Oh, grief, she didn't. 'I'll be busy, I expect,' she answered lamely, but found that Nick was not so easily put off. While he accepted that Saturday evening was out, she would see him again on Sunday, when he came round to do some more decorating?

He walked her to her car and kissed her cheek, and Alethea backed away. Nick Saunders was soon out of her head, however. Had Trent tried to phone?

The phone stayed dead all that weekend. Not that Alethea was in very much. She went to her family home on Saturday morning, and found her mother in a much better humour than when she had last spoken to her. The children seemed better behaved too, or perhaps they were just settling down a little bit more. Even Polly appeared on her best behaviour.

'You didn't say anything about curtains, bed linen or towels, but I've packed a box for you,' Maxine stated as they went round ticking off a list she had suggested.

'I'll let you have everything back,' Alethea promised gratefully. 'As soon as I can get—'

'Don't make it too soon!' Maxine implored, and they both laughed.

With the box of curtains and linen in her boot, Alethea went back to Trent's home thinking that, all in all, it had been a very pleasant day. So why was she feeling more than a little out of sorts?

Trent hadn't phoned. Grief, as if she cared! She didn't *expect* him to ring, for goodness' sake. Heavens above, he had better things to do than to ring her every five minutes!

The decorating really began to take shape on Sunday. She fed Nick a sandwich lunch and cooked an early dinner for both of them on the ancient cooker left behind by the previous tenant, and again worried about Nick doing this work for her. She couldn't offer him money, yet to give him an expensive present seemed much too personal.

She was back in Trent's home by nine-thirty and the phone stayed dead. On Monday, Alethea arranged to have Friday afternoon off work to await the furniture removers. On Tuesday Nick put the finishing touches to her bedroom, and on Thursday he came round to the flat to help her hang the curtains.

Alethea went back to Trent's house; not once that week had he phoned—and she did not care! Why should she? It was ridiculous!

She waited for the furniture to arrive on Friday afternoon, wishing she could feel more excited than she did. She should be ecstatic, for goodness' sake! Her first new home of her own. She should be thrilled and delighted.

True, she couldn't properly move in yet because of Trent, but soon... By her calculations she could expect him home any time after a week today. He'd said he'd be away three weeks, which in actual fact would mean a week on Sunday. But, he might come home a day or two sooner, mightn't he?

The furniture arrived and Alethea went back to Trent's early. She had plenty to do in her flat, but she felt unsettled. She wanted to

be back in the home she shared with him—
only he wasn't there.

On Saturday she decided she'd had enough
of this aching restlessness. She had Nick
Saunders' telephone number, so she picked up
the phone and rang him.

'The least I owe you is a jolly good dinner.
Would you be my guest tonight?' she asked.

'What time?' he asked, before she had
barely finished.

Alethea arranged a time and suggested she
would meet him at the restaurant. But when
Nick insisted he would come and pick her up,
she began to wish she had never phoned him.

She took some clothes round to her flat and
showered and changed there, deciding, since
she had no intention of allowing Nick to drive
her back to Trent's place, she would stay the
night in her own flat.

Nick was a very nice man, the food most
enjoyable and the evening pleasant. It seemed
churlish, since he was so familiar with her flat,
to refuse his suggestion, 'Shall I come in for
coffee?' after the meal. But Alethea was relieved that, having tried to amorously kiss her,

Nick did not pursue it when she turned her face away.

So why was it not Nick's face she saw in her mind's eye when she awakened at her flat on Sunday morning? With Trent in her head the moment she came to, Alethea finally had to give in. This was why she was feeling so lost, so restless, so lonely. She loved the wretched, abominable swine! She didn't want to love him, but she could no longer run away from the truth which had been dogging her.

She was in love with Trent, had been for some while. And he? He couldn't even be bothered to pick up the phone and give her a call!

Alethea left her flat and returned early to Trent's home, but still the phone stayed dead. Well, she didn't care, she told herself. Love him or no, there was still no way she was going to climb into his bed!

She drove to work on Monday feeling thoroughly dispirited and had a panic session: 'Well, I'm glad—no, I'm not.' Perhaps, she wondered, since he hadn't bothered to phone her lately, it meant Trent no longer desired her.

Maybe when he came home at the weekend he would tell her to leave. Perhaps he had found someone he desired more in South America? Oh, go, go, go! She wished with all she had that Trent would go from her heart, and from her head, and so allow her to think of something other than him all the time.

There was a brief respite when Nick Saunders came by her office and, catching her alone, referred to something she had mentioned in passing: the next room she intended to brighten up. 'How about I stop by your place tonight and size up your kitchen?' he suggested.

'Do you mind if I say no?' she asked, still liking him very well, but nowhere near coming to terms with her love for Trent yet, and feeling in the need for some space. 'I'd rather thought of having a rest from decorating this week,' she added quickly, lest he took offence.

'Say when,' he answered, and went on his way. Alethea went back to trying to forget about Trent while she tried to concentrate on her work.

She went home to Trent's house deciding she would have an early night. She supposed she must have slept at some time the previous night, but it hadn't seemed like it.

The phone stayed quiet and she hated him. He was the reason why she was off her food, of course. He was the reason why she couldn't sleep. She tried to damn him—but she loved him.

Loved every tall, broad-shouldered inch of him. He, the lustful rat, all he wanted was her in his bed. Lustful? Could he be called lustful? He hadn't been exactly chasing her around the house brimming with lust, had he? In fact, his kisses had for the most part been more pleasing than panting.

Desiring, then? He desired her in his bed, that was for sure. He'd as good as said so. Well, she wasn't giving in. She glanced at the digital clock; seven minutes past one. Was she never going to go to sleep?

She tried to get comfortable. Up until then her bed had been superb, it suddenly seemed to have rocks in it. She closed her eyes, but was wide awake. She opened them again: eight minutes past one.

Her thoughts went around and around in circles, but she was still no nearer going to sleep. Despite her thoughts not so long ago that she wasn't getting into Trent's bed, she started to get the oddest notion that perhaps she might sleep, feel closer to Trent, if she went and slept in it.

Oh, for goodness' sake! Talk about being mixed-up since she had known him! She closed her eyes again. Then opened them. If she did go and get into his bed, could that be counted as fulfilling her part of the bargain?

She knew it could not, and knew her love for him was making her have some weird ideas. And yet, as minute after wearying minute dragged by, with sleep still evading her, she became so caught up in the need for rest that when the clock showed one fifty-six, Alethea got out of bed and went along the landing to Trent's room.

She opened the door. The room was in darkness but there was enough light from the streetlamps outside for her to make out the double bed. She went over to it. She needed sleep. She felt quite desperately in need of it. In need of rest from her head. Perhaps in Trent's bed she might find the rest she sought.

Alethea hesitated only briefly, then quickly got in. He would never know. She closed her eyes and felt comfortable. A kind of peace washed over her. She snuggled down under the duvet. Trent! Close to him. Her last waking thought was Trent. He would never know.

She had been solidly asleep; she had slept so little just lately. Then something disturbed her. She opened her eyes and was puzzled. There was a small light glowing behind her. She couldn't remember switching on a bedside lamp.

Realising that she must have done, Alethea went to turn over with the intention of switching it off—and nearly fainted with shock. She was not alone in bed.

Jet-propelled, she half sat up, about to rocket from the bed—only Trent was faster. An arm shot out around her and she fought a losing battle trying to get free, not only of his arm but of the tangled up duvet.

'Shh. It's all right. You've nothing to panic about.'

'You shouldn't be here!' she gasped—oh, God, that was his line!

'I'm glad I am,' Trent teased—and she felt an edge of calm. So much for him never knowing that she had slept in his bed!

Although her heart was beating against her ribs ten to the dozen, it was wonderful to see him. Just the mere fact of him being here banished all those lonesome restless emotions that had so achingly plagued her.

'I'd—er—better go,' she mumbled, suddenly starting to become conscious that she was wearing one of her flimsiest nighties and that, in twisting about the way she had, her nightie had twisted too, so that both straps were loose on her shoulders and threatening to fall. That was without mentioning that, when she did take her eyes from Trent's dear face—oh, how she loved him—she realised his chest was naked and he probably hadn't much, if anything, on under the duvet.

But Trent's arm stayed in place around her over the duvet. 'Don't rush off, stay and talk to me for a while,' he urged her calmly.

'It's the middle of the night!'

'If you're going to be precise about it, it's ten past three in the morning.'

'There you are!' she exclaimed, and made another unsuccessful attempt to get free of his arm, before curiosity got the better of her. 'I didn't expect you home before the weekend. You said you'd be away three weeks.'

'I finished my work sooner than expected and caught an earlier flight.'

'Oh, are you hungry?' she asked, getting some weird idea that to go to the kitchen to fix him something would be a way of getting out of this room with her dignity intact.

'I could be. What are you offering?' he asked politely. But, on looking into his eyes, Alethea saw that there was mischief dancing there.

'Oh, you!' she grumbled impatiently.

How in creation was she going to get back to her own room with her skimpy nightie riding up around her thighs! To complete her embarrassment, one of her shoulder straps chose just that precise moment to flop down.

Before she could reach it, however, Trent's hand was there, pushing the offending strap back in place. 'Thank you,' she murmured chokily, a tingle shooting through her at his touch. She desperately needed to get out of

his bed, out of his room. Yet, even more desperately, as a face-saving exercise, she needed
a reason for being in his bed in the first place.
Hot-water bottle burst? In the heat of
summer! 'I—er—hope you don't mind me
using your—er—bed,' she began.

'I've been hoping for it,' Trent answered,
and she loved him so much. Even when there
must be questions he could find to ask, he
was not asking them. Plus, when the situation
she was in offered him everything, he was not
taking advantage, but was staying teasing,
good-humoured.

'It's the first time I've used your bed,' she
informed him by the way of an explanation.

She loved him all the more when, as easily
as before, he instructed her gently, 'Don't
worry about it. There isn't a problem.' Oh,
Trent! Then he smiled. 'I've been—looking
forward to seeing you. It's a bonus to have
you here to talk to and not have to wait until
morning to see you.'

He could have no idea what it meant to her
to hear him say he had been looking forward
to seeing her. 'That's... Well...' She coughed,
and tried to string another sentence together.

If only she'd thought to bring her housecoat with her! But she hadn't, and if she went to snatch the duvet off him to drape it around herself, then she was fairly sure that would leave him stark naked. Oh, grief, grief, grief! 'I don't suppose you'll be going to work very early, but—um—I'll have to be up at my usual time,' she tried, adding primly, 'If you'd like to put the light out, I'll...'

'Oh, Miss Modesty, you're wonderful,' Trent tormented her. She couldn't take any more of it. Flimsy nightie or not, she was leaving. She went to get out of bed in a rush, but was again stopped as Trent relented and, placing a warm hand on her shoulder, asked, 'Before you go, may I have a hello kiss?'

With his hand burning on her shoulder, Alethea couldn't find her voice to answer. Trent took her silence to mean that she had no objection. She felt the pressure of his hand on her shoulder increase and knew as his head started to come nearer that she wanted him to kiss her; she was starved for his kisses.

Which was probably why what should have been a brief kiss of greeting became more than a mere touching of lips. For, as his mouth touched hers, Alethea raised a hand to his shoulder and found she could not push him away—she did not want to push him away. And it seemed while she could not pull away, Trent could not break from her either.

She heard him give a strangled kind of groan, then, while they were both sitting there in that big bed, Trent gathered her into his arms, and their kiss deepened.

All her thinking power departed as Trent held her close. Alethea clung to him. She had missed him, missed him so much. She loved him; nothing else mattered.

Trent kissed her again, more deeply this time, and her heart started to sing. She kissed him back. Held onto him as his hands caressed her back. It was bliss to let her hands rove too, feeling muscle, skin, warmth.

Again he kissed her and, while clinging to him, she was only vaguely aware that the straps of her nightdress presented no problem to his scientific mind. Unexpectedly, she realised it was around her waist; the top half of her was as uncovered as Trent's.

'Sweet Alethea,' he breathed, pulling her close up against him. She heard him groan again when her warm, swollen breasts came up against his hair-tufted chest. 'Alethea, Alethea.' He called her name and she gloried in the feel of him.

With the next kiss he moved her a little away from him, but only so that his hands and sensitive fingers could caress the front of her. She felt him capture her breasts and she wanted more—much, much more.

'Trent,' she cried his name.

'Don't be alarmed,' he breathed gently, his mouth moving to her ear.

I'm not alarmed, she wanted to tell him, but couldn't, so she bent her head and kissed his neck. She felt his grip on her tighten and she had an urge to stroke his chest.

She bent her head, and he pulled back a little to allow her access to whatever pleased her. Alethea kissed his nipples; it seemed right to do so. Then she raised her tousled blonde head and found she was looking, quite unashamedly, into Trent's dark eyes—eyes that seemed to smoulder fiercely with barely checked desire.

'You're so beautiful,' he breathed, then, as if he needed to be even closer to her, he manoeuvred her to lie down and, with his warm, naked body half covering her, he kissed her.

The fire in her spiralled out of control when Trent transferred his kisses to the pink-tipped hardened peaks of her breasts. Somehow her nightdress had disappeared from her waist and she knew herself to be as naked as he.

His kisses, the erotic movements of his mouth over her breast as he captured some of its fullness in his mouth, moulded it with his tongue before slowing, allowing it to slide away, then capturing it again, and once more slowly letting her breast glide from the warm firmness of his mouth, caused her to be unaware of anything save him and this urgent need he had aroused in her.

She knew that she wanted him, was his for the taking. Indeed, she felt she would beg him to take her if he did not do so soon. But, when Trent stopped tantalising her breast with his mouth and kissed her, while she held onto him and gloried that the supreme moment would soon be here, and Trent placed a caressing hand on her behind and eased her back against him, some belated modesty caused her to jerk back.

'I'm sorry,' she said at once, and would have gone on to ask Trent to forgive that moment of shyness, only suddenly he stilled and, instead of pulling her close up against him as she anticipated he would, he gave a groan of a sound, let go of her and moved from her.

She didn't understand it, nor did she understand it when he moved further away, no part of their bodies touching now, and sat up.

'H-have I offended you?' she asked, and loved him so. As he looked down at her and then to her hardened pink-tipped breasts fully exposed to his view, he took hold of the duvet and tenderly covered her from his gaze. But she loved him.

'Alethea,' he said slowly; he still desired her; she just knew it. 'That was one hell of a kiss hello.' He paused for a brief moment, then went firmly on, 'But, as you yourself said, you have to be up for work in a few hours' time.'

She stared at him, not comprehending. She was quite desperate for him and she was sure he wanted her. 'I . . .' she began, on her way to telling him that she did not understand. But Trent turned from her.

She watched as he switched off the bedside lamp—it was as if he had slapped her. She, in her naïveté, had got it wrong. He had wanted her, but no longer did. Trent wasn't verbally telling her to get out of his bed but, by switching off that lamp, was intent on making it easy for her to leave.

She was certain of it when, as she turned back the duvet, he made no attempt to stop her from leaving. She felt too choked to speak. She left, went quickly, fearing her pride might be split asunder if she could not hold down her tears before she got to her room.

CHAPTER EIGHT

ALETHEA did not cry, though she came exceedingly close. Back in her room she snatched a fresh nightdress from a drawer and got into bed, but she did not sleep. How could she sleep? She had much too much on her mind.

Over and over again she relived how willingly, how ardently she had returned Trent's kisses. There could not have been the smallest shred of doubt in his mind that she had wanted him to make love to her.

And what had been his response? After making her barely restrained with need for him, he had moved away from her. 'You have to be up for work in a few hours' time,' he had reminded her.

But the whole point of her living in his home was because he wanted her in his bed. So why, by virtue of switching off that table-lamp, had he turfed her out of it?

It didn't make sense. Why would...? Abruptly her thoughts stopped. She gasped and nearly sank under the enormity of what had just come to her. It didn't make sense—unless Trent had suddenly realised that she was head over heels in love with him.

Oh, no! Everything in her shied away from that possibility. But the more she thought about it, the more it made sense. He had desired her; she knew that without question. So why else, when—shaming but true—she had been his for the taking, had he decided to deny his own need? Lord, Trent hadn't been looking for *that* sort of complication. To have her fall in love with him was something for which he would have no time.

Alethea was still in the agonising throes of trying to believe that she had not given herself away, when her alarm went off.

Quickly she silenced it, not wanting to disturb Trent in the next-door room. Then she heard a sound that told her Trent was already awake. She realised that the sound she heard came not from Trent's room, but from the door of her own.

And Alethea, save for being aware that she had suddenly gone scarlet, didn't quite know how she felt when Trent entered her room.

He was robe-clad, and came towards her bearing a cup of tea on a tray. 'You should be asleep!' She found her voice in a hurry as he put down the tray.

'That's the thanks I get,' he drawled easily, his eyes on her as he came and sat on the edge of her bed.

Her heart was thundering away but she made herself meet his eyes. 'Thank you,' she mumbled, and all at once became aware that the nightdress she had on covered her little better than the one she had left in his room.

Hurriedly she tugged the duvet higher up her chest, and came close to disliking Trent de Havilland when she observed he was watching her attempt to cover herself with some amusement. Oh, that she'd been so modest last night!

'You're sensational, even when you're blushing,' he said gently.

'Trent, I...' Oh, grief, her brain was all over the place. What could she say?

'I shouldn't tease you.' He saved her from having to say anything. But he managed to terrify her nonetheless when his teasing manner was replaced by a deadly serious look. 'Alethea, I think we should talk.'

Oh, no! He knew that she loved him! Or, did he? Some part of her brain activated sufficiently for her to be able to reason that, since Trent wasn't telling her to pack her bags and leave, but was saying they should talk, perhaps he hadn't seen how she had fallen so utterly to pieces over him.

But her nerves were still jumping and she couldn't think very straight. She needed to think. 'I have to be at work for nine,' she said on a rush. She wasn't ready to talk. In fact, she doubted that she ever would be ready.

'Not now,' Trent agreed. Clearly, whatever it was he thought they should talk about, he wasn't about to have any kind of hurried conversation. 'Tonight,' he decreed, without compromise.

'Er—very well,' Alethea agreed. And weathered his long, hard stare, before he got up and left her to it.

Alethea didn't know whether she was glad or sorry that that Tuesday at her office proved so busy she was fully occupied with work problems and had no time to give consideration to her own.

At ten past five Carol Robinson put down her pen. 'Flap over!' she smiled at Alethea. 'What a day!'

'I've known quieter ones,' Alethea agreed as they tidied their desks.

She was in her car and on her way to Trent's home when she all at once knew that she wasn't ready to see him yet. She wasn't ready to talk, not until she'd had some time to try and analyse what it was he wanted to talk about.

She had detoured to her basement flat before she could think further. She made herself a cup of Earl Grey tea and sat down, stood up, and then started to walk around restlessly. She needed calm. An hour went by, but her thoughts were still going around in the same wearying circle.

Trent was sharp, astute. Oh, *had* she given away that she loved him? She would like to think that she hadn't. But she just didn't know. Another hour went by.

Her tea was stone-cold. She went and made another cup. Knowing Trent, despite not having flown in until the early hours—oh, she didn't want to be reminded!—he would probably still show his face at his office that day. And, knowing the work hours he kept, he wouldn't be home for ages yet...

Someone ringing her doorbell startled her out of her thoughts. Oh, grief. She did hope it wasn't Nick. Not that she'd arranged to see him. She needed space. Perhaps it was a neighbour come to pay a friendly visit. She hadn't met any of her neighbours yet.

Alethea went to the door—and nearly dropped with shock. It wasn't Nick and it wasn't a neighbour. 'Trent!' she exclaimed, not sure she wasn't crimson again. Her insides were an instant clamour, that was for certain. 'Er—come in,' she invited belatedly, standing back. What was he doing there? The question screamed in her brain as, fumbling the catch, she closed the door and led the way into her sitting room. At that precise moment she couldn't ever remember telling him where her flat was!

'You seem to be comfortably settled here,' he commented evenly.

Was there an underlying tough note there? As if he wasn't exactly thrilled to have to come looking for her? Her heartbeat quickened— what *did* he want to talk about that was so important? Something that meant he'd come here rather than wait? 'Ac-actually, it's Maxine's furniture—mostly,' she said nervously. 'She said I—' She broke off, realising she was babbling on. Swiftly she did what she could to get a grip on herself. 'Um—did I tell you where this flat was?'

Trent scrutinised her face, seeming to note every nuance in her expression. She felt vulnerable, wide open. 'You didn't—your sister did.'

'My s... Maxine. You've been in touch with Maxine?' Alethea stared at him incredulously.

'I thought I might when you showed no signs of coming home,' he answered succinctly.

'You rang her?' Alethea asked quickly, not caring particularly what she said, provided it kept him from wondering why she hadn't gone straight back to his place.

'I rang your old home. Your sister answered and said you didn't live there any more.'

'She gave you this address without question?'

'I explained I'd been out of the country for a while and would like to contact you. Your sister seemed to think she owed me a small favour.' Bearing in mind what Trent had done for Maxine and her family, a small favour was the least Maxine owed him. But... 'Tell me, Alethea—what are you afraid of?' he asked.

Open-mouthed, decidedly jittery, she stared at him. He was calm and she was terrified. 'N-nothing,' she replied, wanting to be a million miles away.

'Don't lie. You're—' He broke off as someone rang her doorbell. Never had a caller, whoever it was, been more welcome to her.

'Excuse me,' she said in a rush, and went quickly out into the small hallway, only to find Nick Saunders, wine bottle in hand, was just closing her front door behind him.

'Your door wasn't fully closed,' he said, by way of explanation for letting himself in. And, beaming broadly, he held the wine bottle aloft. 'I thought we might celebrate our efforts in your bedroom. That is...' A roar of a sound from the sitting room caused Alethea to have very rapid second thoughts about her caller being welcome. A split second later, an enraged Trent de Havilland joined them.

'Who the hell are you?' he demanded of her visitor before she had chance to so much as think of performing any introductions. Trent looked ready to flatten Nick if he wasn't fast enough with his answers.

Nick seemed shaken rigid to find a man he didn't know so unexpectedly in Alethea's home. 'Nick Saunders,' he replied. 'I'm a friend...who are you?' he got his second wind to return.

Oh, grief, Trent wasn't looking any sweeter. But since he hadn't flattened Nick yet, there was hope. Or was there? Alethea was ready to do some flattening herself when, without mincing words, Trent snarled, 'I just happen to be the man Miss Pemberton lives with.'

She gasped and Nick looked astounded. 'You're *living* with someone?' he asked, staggered. What could she say? Not a thing, Alethea realised. 'But—last week ...'

'I was away on business last week!' Trent clipped, not allowing him to finish.

Nick was still looking thunderstruck. 'Is— is this true?' he asked her. There was no way she could deny any of it.

'Yes,' she mumbled, feeling miserable and starting to hate Trent de Havilland.

But Nick already had his answer: she wasn't arguing.

'Thanks!' he offered sourly, and went.

Alethea felt dreadful—and angry. She turned to Trent and exploded. 'Thanks a million!'

He ignored her anger. 'Am I missing something here?' he questioned curtly.

'Not a thing!' she retorted.

'Then how come, when I have to ring your sister to find out this address, Bacchus there not only knew it, but seemed to think celebrations were in order for what the two of you got up to in your bedroom!'

Dearly would she have loved to tell him to go to hell, but, for all Trent now seemed to have his fury under tight control, he still appeared to be enraged enough to strangle her if she said anything provocative.

'I should think you, more than anyone, know me better than that!' She flew at him, and nearly died when she realised that, after the abandoned way she'd been with him last night, that was no reference. 'For your information,' she charged on, refusing to let him or her memories sink her, 'Nick helped me decorate the bedroom. In fact he did the lion's share of the work. It was a foul colour!'

'How kind!' Sarcastic brute! 'Did he also help you to move your bedroom furniture in too?'

'The furniture removers did that last Friday.'

'And you invited him round tonight for a cosy——'

'No, I did *not*!' she blazed. Dammit, she'd done nothing wrong. But he had! Trent-tell-the-world-de Havilland had. 'Did you have to make me look so—so cheap?' she challenged furiously. 'Did you...?'

'Cheap? What the hell did I say to—?'

'Nick Saunders works at Gale Drilling!' she erupted, refusing to allow Trent sole rights to butting-in. 'By telling him, you've most likely informed everyone I work with that I live with you! Everyone at—'

'And that makes you feel cheap?' Trent cut in, his fury clearly on the rampage again. 'Living with me makes you feel cheap?' he challenged, hell bent on an answer, it seemed.

'How else would I feel?' She refused to back down. 'I should brag about living with you? Tell everybody of my great good fortune that—?' She broke off; she could tell by the narrowing of Trent's eyes, by the taut anger in him, that she had gone too far, but she didn't seem able to stop. 'You think that to be your mistress is the be-all and end-all of my existence. Well, it isn't—and as soon as I can be free of you, I'll—'

Trent stopped her right there. 'Consider it done!' he snarled. 'As yet, you haven't been my mistress, but if it cheapens you so much, then to hell with you! You stay here, sweetheart!' he gritted. 'You needn't even come back to pick up your belongings—I'll have them sent round!' With that, he brushed past her and she was left staring after him.

She cried. Pig, swine, pig. It was over, and she had never felt so unhappy in her life. Abruptly her anger at Trent evaporated. But it was too late to take back any of the things she had said.

Alethea went to work the next morning in low spirits, and during a lull in that morning's work, she left her desk and went along to Nick Saunders' office. She wasn't looking forward to it, but after his goodness she felt she owed him some sort of an explanation.

Thankfully he was in his office on his own. 'Nick. I'm sorry. I owe you an apology,' was the best she could do.

'I'd have appreciated you telling me about your man-friend, rather than letting me find out the way I did,' Nick answered, leaving his desk and coming over to her.

'It—wasn't very—nice of me, was it?' she agreed. It wouldn't make it any less honest to say that she'd never dreamed that Trent would turn up at her flat.

'You're in love with him?'

She nodded, adding, 'We're—um—going through a difficult patch just now.'

'Which is why you've found somewhere else to live—a sort of retreat?' She said nothing, but felt she had never liked Nick so well when he commented, 'I suppose it would have been something of a miracle if there hadn't been some man around in the background somewhere.' She smiled at him, and felt a whole lot better about the embarrassment she had caused him when he smiled back. 'Tell you what, lovely Alethea,' he said then, 'if you ever dump him, just let me be the second to know.'

Alethea went back to her own office. Dump Trent! She reckoned it would be a first if any female lasted with Trent long enough to try it.

There were no suitcases waiting for her when she returned to her flat, and she spent the entire evening on the edge of her seat, listening for the sound of someone delivering her luggage. She hadn't truly expected that Trent would call again in person. Nor did he. In fact no one called, and she eventually took herself off to bed, wanting quite desperately to see Trent again but knowing that she must accept that it was over.

During her lunch hour on Thursday, Alethea purchased a blouse and some underwear. She went home that night to find that her belongings had still not arrived. The rest of the evening followed the same dull pattern as previously.

Alethea determined on Friday that she was just not going to spend another long evening watching each heartsick minute drag by. She made a brief stop at her flat—still no delivery—and drove to her mother's home. She still had a few clothes there. If her possessions left at Trent's home didn't soon materialise, she was going to need them.

Funny that, she mused as she drove along. Judging by the way Trent had been on Tuesday—enraged was not the word for it!—she'd have thought her belongings would have been hurled at her door within an hour of him leaving!

Maxine and her daughters were delighted to see her, and her mother seemed to be making an effort to keep her acid remarks down to a minimum. 'I thought it about time

I collected the rest of my clothes,' Alethea mentioned as she sat drinking tea, knowing without ill feeling that, no matter how down she felt just then, she had made the right decision to leave her mother's home.

'I'll come and help you, if you like,' Maxine volunteered.

'And me!' piped up two small voices.

'I thought you were going to read a story with Nanna,' Maxine reminded them.

'Polly's excelling herself,' Alethea remarked. Having lost the two elder children to their grandmother, she, Maxine and Polly went up the stairs.

'Don't!' Maxine hushed her.

Alethea laughed. She hadn't tempted fate too far, she discovered, because Polly remained angelic as they folded and bagged the articles of clothing she had left behind.

'Has Trent de Havilland been in touch?' Maxine asked.

Alethea nodded. 'Thanks for giving him my address,' she added lightly.

'You didn't mind? I felt I...'

'I'm glad you did,' Alethea assured her, but did not, could not, discuss it or him. 'How are things with you?' she asked.

'Getting better by the day,' Maxine smiled. 'Believe it or not, when Mother forgets to be sour, she's brilliant with Sadie and Georgia. There's a buyer for the house, and I've started receiving maintenance from Keith.'

'He's got another job?'

'A good one. It's in the Middle East—not the same work he was doing but it pays well.'

Alethea vaguely remembered that Keith had acquired a degree in civil engineering or something similar before he'd gone into finance. Perhaps there would be less temptation in civil engineering.

At her mother's invitation she stayed to dinner, but drove back to her flat afterwards with Trent, as ever, in her mind. It occurred briefly to her to wonder if, since she had not made love with him ... Alethea felt herself go pink; that had been solely his decision—my stars, she had been willing enough! Since she hadn't made love with him, might Trent consider any agreement not to prosecute her brother-in-law null and void? But, she had wondered only briefly. Somehow, she realised, she trusted Trent. Somehow, no matter what went on between her and Trent—or in this case, what hadn't gone on—she just instinctively knew that he had not picked up his phone to ring his lawyers.

Trent was still in her head on Saturday. He had wanted to talk to her, for them to talk, he'd said. Alethea swallowed hard. Whatever it was he had thought they had to talk about, she could guarantee the subject had long since been consigned to the waste-bin.

That Saturday seemed to go on for ever. She didn't go out all day, and he did not call. She wondered when, if ever, this aching emptiness would get any better?

On Sunday it was still there. As she had so many times, she went over again that last time she had seen Trent. Oh, how could she ever have accused him of making her look cheap?

So much for fearing he might have gleaned how she felt about him. She guessed that her 'cheap' comments had firmly hit on the head any notion he might have nursed that she was in love with him.

And, while she was heartily glad that her pride was saved in that direction, Alethea at last owned that, when once she had wanted a place of her own, now it was not what she wanted at all. What she wanted was to live with Trent.

Alethea knew then, as she supposed she had known from the time Trent had left last Tuesday, that he would not be calling at her flat again.

Having been away in South America for a couple of weeks, he'd probably had a heavy workload to catch up on. It was painful to her to think of him leaving home so early in the morning and returning late in the evening. She wished she was there to look after him; not that he'd let her—he'd most likely die laughing at the very idea. Though if he was putting in all those hours, there would be little time left over to think of bundling her gear into a couple of cases and having them sent over in a taxi.

Alethea resigned herself to hoping that Trent would get around to gathering her belongings together at some time next week. Unless... Unless, of course... She made

herself finish the staggering sentence that
pushed to be admitted. Unless she saved him
the bother and went to his home and did it
for herself! She took a shaky breath. Why
shouldn't she go over and collect...? In an
instant she dismissed the idea. Grief, as if she
would! For Heaven's sake, had she no more
pride than that? She faced that pride took a
hammering when placed up against her
longing to see Trent again. But, really, she
would stop thinking such nonsensical
thoughts at once!

And yet, throughout Sunday, the notion
once born stubbornly refused to go away. It
plagued her, made her cross with herself that
she, a fairly intelligent person, seemed incapable of thinking beyond Trent. Trent!
Trent-get-out-of-my-head-de Havilland.

She took herself off for a walk, and found
she was silently arguing with herself. Why
shouldn't she go round to Trent's house for
her clothes? They were hers, and she could do
with a change of business suit.

Having counter-argued that she'd buy
another suit, she returned to her flat. Now she
was thinking along the lines that he probably

wouldn't be in even if she did go round. He worked hard; he was probably playing hard at this very minute.

She didn't like her following thought: doubtless there'd be some sensational-looking female helping him play! But she dismissed such painful images. She had a key, didn't she? No way, she determined firmly.

It was early evening when Alethea knew she could take no more. Thoughts of Trent, her need to see him, the things she had left behind, had bombarded her all day. Pride just didn't enter into it any more. She needed action. She had to go, if only to know that she had achieved something.

She was in her car and on her way to Trent's home when nerves started to bite and she hoped Trent was not in. Perhaps he'd gone abroad again.

Alethea was pulling up outside his house when she had the most diabolical thought: perhaps he wasn't out, but in, entertaining some woman-friend! She almost pressed her foot hard on the accelerator and shot past where he lived.

But, being so close to his home, so close to where he might be, somehow she just could not do it. Someone else seemed to be in charge of her as she got out of her car and went up the steps to Trent's front door.

That person was still in charge of her when, feeling it would be an intrusion to use her key and walk straight in, she rang his doorbell. Then she immediately wanted to run. She should have phoned first; he wasn't in—oh, God, somebody was coming!

CHAPTER NINE

ALETHEA was a quivering mass of nerves
when, after seeming to take forever to be
opened, the front door was pulled back.
Trent! For several seconds she was too
emotionally full to be able to utter a word. It
was just plain wonderful to see him.

But Trent, his unsmiling expression telling
her nothing, appeared to have little he wanted
to say. He had not a word of greeting, nor
did he tell her to get lost, either. But, with his
dark eyes looking nowhere but at her face, he
just stood there.

Striving with all she had to get herself under
control, she blurted out in a sudden rush,
'Is it convenient? Are you entertaining? I
sh-should have telephoned first.' Oh, Lord,
she was gabbling. He was nobody's fool. He'd
know she was nervous. 'I'll—er—come back
later,' she uttered in a breathless sentence, and
had half turned from the front door when,
moving with lightning speed, Trent stepped

231

forward and caught her arm in a detaining hold.

'You might as well come in now that you're here,' he remarked smoothly, and Alethea felt his firm hold on her arm tighten, urging her towards him and over his threshold.

'Am—I—interrupting   anything?'   she asked jerkily as he closed the door after her and let go of her arm.

'Not a thing,' he replied evenly, ushering her into the drawing room.

'I don't want to intrude. I can just go up for my things if you...'

'You're not intruding, Alethea,' he cut in pleasantly. 'Your belongings can wait for a while. Take a seat and tell me what you've been doing this last few days.'

To tell him about her recent activities would bore him out of his skull. But, and she knew she was being weak, Alethea went over to one of the sofas and sat down. 'I—er—haven't been doing anything very exciting,' she mumbled, looking around the room which, in so short a time, had become very familiar to her, but which she now wanted to photograph in her mind. Self-inflicted punishment it might be, but she wanted to imagine Trent in this room, on that sofa opposite...

'You've not been out for an evening?'

He was merely being polite; she knew that. 'I went to my mother's on Friday.'

'How was she?'

'You care?'

He laughed, and she loved him, and suddenly she started to feel a little better. 'Can I get you a drink? A coffee?' he offered.

'Nothing, thanks.' She didn't seem to be able to remember a time when she had never loved him. 'You've been busy, I expect.'

He shrugged. 'You know how it is,' he answered, using the arm of the other sofa for a seat.

She might be feeling a trifle more relaxed, but suddenly she ran out of polite conversation. 'I'd better go upstairs and—' She didn't get to finish.

'I think we should have our talk first,' Trent cut her off shortly.

She stared at him in consternation. Clearly he had got tired of small talk too. But, by that criteria, did he now mean he wanted them to talk in depth? He had said, on Tuesday morning, that he thought they should talk. All her fears rushed back with a vengeance. 'I thought—I didn't think—n-now, after... I thought that there was not now anything to talk about. Everything seems to me to be resolved.' She shouldn't have come. Oh, where had her brain been? Why had she so let her emotions lead her?

'We've resolved nothing,' Trent said evenly.

Alethea was a seething mass of panic inside that he might have seen her love for him. 'Oh,' she murmured while trying desperately to cope. 'I—um—' She broke off. Trent could be tough, she knew that, but he wasn't a cruel man. He wouldn't deliberately want to bring up the subject of how she felt about him for the pure hell of it, would he? Because she had offended him by telling him he had made her feel cheap, would he? Surely, now that she no longer lived with him... Her thoughts stopped right there—and went up another avenue. 'Has this anything to do with my brother-in-law?' she asked abruptly.

'Your brother-in-law?' He seemed puzzled.

Alethea, for all she was still feeling extremely nervous, just had to give a small

smile. 'I didn't think it had, that you—'
Again she broke off, realising Trent would
think she was talking in riddles. 'I wondered,
though only briefly and not very seriously,
if—with me not living with you now and—
er—everything—if you might feel I'd broken
the agreement we made with—er—regard to
Keith Lawrence's non-prosecution,' she
managed in something of a staccato fashion.

'At least you trust me sufficiently not to
give that matter more than brief consideration,' Trent replied drily. But he looked, she
thought, to be encouraged by her remarks.
What he'd got to be encouraged about,
however, was a mystery to her. But, after
looking at her long and levelly for some moments, he added, 'The issue of your brother-
in-law, my dear Alethea, ceased to be of importance some while back.'

Strangely, then, she gained the oddest
notion that Trent seemed as tense as she was!
Ridiculous! What had he got to be tense
about? For goodness' sake, get your head
together. Trent was sharp; she knew that.
'It—did?' she questioned edgily. She wasn't
sure that she liked that 'my dear Alethea'

either. It hadn't sounded much like an endearment. Oh, get your head together, do.
Why *would* it sound like an endearment?

'It was of importance to start with,' Trent
agreed, though she was a little lost by now.
'But the issue at this moment...' He paused,
and then very deliberately added, 'Is you, and
me.'

Terror-stricken, she almost stood up in her
panic. But, by some great fortune, she managed not to, didn't give away that she was in
something of a blue funk.

'I see,' she lied. Realising that, if she was
to get out of there with any small degree of
pride, she must head him off from finding any
confirmation that she loved him, she said, 'I
was rather rude with my remark—er—at my
flat last Tuesday...'

'That I'd made you look cheap?' He'd remembered! Not that she had expected him to
have forgotten a thing like that.

'I'm sorry. I'm sorry I said it,' she apologised, as she knew she ought.

'You didn't mean it?'

This time she wanted to be truthful. 'I think
it was more that...well, while I know the

world and his wife, or maybe not his wife,' she faltered, 'lives together these days, I'd never done it before. And—um—perhaps the way I was brought up had something to do with it. I don't know, but, while it never troubled me that you and I knew I was living here, I hadn't—um—adjusted yet to telling anyone else that I was living with someone. I'm telling this very badly.'

'That's because you're feeling a little uneasy.'

'You guessed,' she answered miserably.

'If it's any comfort, I'm not feeling so self-assured as I'm striving to sound,' Trent owned up, to her amazement.

Alethea's violet eyes shot wide. She didn't believe that for a second. Trent was always supremely self-assured. But yet... There was something, something indefinable in the stiffness of his back perhaps, a tautness in the way he was sitting, that suggested... Was she crazy? 'Wh-what have you got to be nervous about?' she asked.

'This talk,' he admitted at once. 'This talk which I believed on Tuesday morning, and still believe now, we have gone too far not to have.'

Her thoughts flashed back to Tuesday morning. Early on Tuesday morning she had been his for the taking, but he had rejected the offer. 'You're sure you wouldn't prefer I just went upstairs for my stuff, and quietly got out of here?'

'I've never been more certain about any-thing,' he replied firmly—which defeated her totally. Why, in that case, should he be one whit nervous?

Oh, Heavens. He looked so determined. She wanted to swallow, but wouldn't. That he felt they had gone too far not to have this 'talk' bothered her a great deal. And yet, there was a wayward part of her that wanted to stay and hear what he had to say. A part of her that started to feel that—provided Trent kept away from the subject of what had happened when he had come home from South America and had found her in his bed—she might just manage to weather this 'talk'.

'Er—where would you like to start?'

Trent eyed her without speaking for some seconds, but, as her nerves began to bite afresh, he finally answered, 'Where we met, I think.'

'Mr and Mrs Chapman's silver wedding celebration?' That sounded fairly safe. 'You came over and introduced yourself.'

'I'd been watching the changing expressions on your face for some while.' His gaze was fixed on her as he quietly added, 'I thought you the most beautiful woman I had ever seen.'

Her eyes widened, her mouth went dry. She wanted to say something in reply, but what did she say when the man she loved with her whole heart had just stated that he'd thought her most beautiful? 'We danced,' was what she did say.

'Oh, we did,' he murmured. 'And I shall never forget holding you, warm, alive, exquisite in my arms.' Her eyes widened even further, and she wasn't sure her jaw hadn't dropped. She would never forget Trent holding her close, nor that breathless, tingling feeling that had come over her.

'I—er—think you must have left shortly afterwards,' Alethea commented, feeling a need to say something, but fighting to keep her brain clear. Trent was still a master at confusing her.

He looked pleased. 'You noticed?' Oh, grief—she was going to have to watch her every word!

'Now and then,' she trotted out in light, off-hand fashion. She saw the corners of his mouth twitch, and was ready to get up and leave.

Only she stayed. And she was glad she was still there when Trent very nearly electrified her. He went on, 'I couldn't stay, Alethea. I'm a hard-headed man of science, a logical thinker, I'd always believed. Yet there I was: one sight of you, one dance with you, and I was immediately soft in the head and totally incapable of thinking logically.'

She stared at him dumbstruck. Large-eyed, solemn-expressioned, she was incapable of looking away. 'You—confused me, a lot,' she commented chokily, and, confused again, was barely aware that she had spoken. But, sorely needing cover as she started to remember that Trent had wanted her to live with him because he desired her, she—and she accepted that she wasn't too well educated in such matters—

realised that male desire must have a tremendous impact if it had rendered Trent incapable of thinking logically.

He leaned forward. Instinctively, she pulled back. 'I won't harm you,' he assured her quickly.

He was too late with that assurance. She was harmed, and hurting. But her thoughts were private, her own, and she didn't want him locking on to her hurt. In an attempt to deflect him, she said in a rush, 'You rang me. A couple of days later, you rang me.' She slowed down, but still felt a need to deflect him as she tacked on, 'You rang and asked me out to dinner.'

'Not giving you chance to say no.'

He *was* deflected. She started to breathe more easily. 'I intended to ring you the next day to say I couldn't make it,' she admitted. 'Only I didn't know where you worked. I didn't know then that you had your own firm. Anyhow, the day got away from me rather, and—' She broke off, aware that she was gabbling again. 'And you called for me,' she ended lamely.

'And found out so much about you, and your family, that evening,' he inserted quietly.

She hadn't thought he'd found out all that much about her. 'I'm not going to apologise for my family,' she stated, perhaps a touch sharply.

'I shouldn't want you to,' he disarmed her immediately.

She instantly softened. 'Well, perhaps for my brother-in-law,' she reconsidered.

'Whatever you do, don't apologise for him,' Trent quickly instructed. 'Without him, I'd have had a much tougher time than I'm having in what I set out to achieve.'

'You'll be sending him a thank-you note next!' Alethea erupted waspishly. So, all right, she accepted that her nerves were jumpy, but, if she remembered it correctly, what Trent had set out to achieve was to get her in his bed. Well, she'd been in his bed, and he'd turned her down!

'Oh, my word,' Trent interrupted her unhappy thoughts. 'Mine aren't the only raw nerves around here.'

'Hmmph!' she scorned. But curiosity was starting to get the better of her. 'The way I heard it,' she started, 'if I didn't give my answer to your—er—proposition in a very short time, your legal department were going to have Keith Lawrence's blood, so...' Her voice tailed off and her heart started to pound. 'What—?' She broke off again, and felt utterly lost. It seemed Trent was *pleased* that her brother-in-law had robbed him. 'I'm confused again,' she owned.

'It's my fault.' To her amazement Trent at once took the blame. 'I'm trying, with what clear thinking you've left me...' she blinked at that but he was going on '...to clear everything up, take out the dead wood so that...' He looked from her as if searching for the right words—only her brain was still trying to cope with his statement: 'what clear thinking you've left me...'!

'We—er—seemed to be getting a bit bogged down,' she offered, because she wanted to help him out while, at the same time, she was still determined that he must not see anything of her love for him; she was still hoping that he hadn't guessed at her feelings. 'Look, our—er—um—talk doesn't seem . . . I mean, if you'd like to cancel it, I'll g—'

'No way!' he cut in bluntly. 'I'm sorry,' he apologised, but she was unsure what he was apologising for—his bluntness or the fact that the talk they were having didn't seem to be getting off the ground. 'Forgive me, my dear,' he requested, and while she was still recovering after this man, whom she knew to hold endearments in short supply, had twice in the space of fifteen minutes called her 'my dear', he was explaining, 'I've rehearsed this over and over and it still isn't coming out right.'

Her violet eyes were huge in her face. He really did sound as though he was under a great deal of strain! She had no clue as to what he had rehearsed, but, again because of the love she bore for him, she had to try to ease matters for him. 'Would it help if you forgot what you've rehearsed and just said straight out what it is that—er—troubles you?' she suggested.

Trent's dark eyes scrutinised her sensitive expression, then he smiled, a gentle kind of smile. 'You trouble me, Alethea Pemberton,' he said. 'You have from the beginning.'

'Oh,' she mumbled, her heart racing.

'And, to tell it straight out...' He hesitated. 'Already I'm losing my nerve.'

'I don't believe it! You're always so—so confident about everything.'

'I wish I had your belief about that,' he commented. And, taking what seemed to be a long and steadying breath, he confessed, 'To tell it like it is, I'll have to confess that I found reason to be grateful to your brother-in-law.'

'But—he robbed you!'

'He was also instrumental in bringing you to my door. Had it not been because of him you would never have taken up my invitation to a non-existent gathering that Saturday night.'

'Non-existent?' she queried. 'Your friends were stranded in Paris. You said...'

'I lied.'

'You lied?' she gasped. 'You...'

'I had to,' he confirmed. 'Alethea, my dear Alethea.' Oh, help her! Her heart was going to leap straight out of her body if he didn't pack this up! That look, that tone! 'I'd been in Italy on business for a couple of days. I got back on the Friday and...' he paused, but his eyes were steady on hers when he resumed, 'And felt such a longing to see you that I phoned you, intending to ask you out that night. But it was plain, before I could so much as ask, that you already had a date that evening.'

'I didn't,' she answered without thinking, her thoughts still with those magical words: Trent had been longing to see her. Was that what pure physical desire did for you? Or dared she begin to hope...? Oh, don't be ridiculous, of course it was pure physical desire, and only...

'You lied?'

'D-did I?' She was too churned up inside to be able to remember.

'You—intimated,' he corrected, 'that you'd got a date. And, to put it mildly, I found that very upsetting.'

'Upsetting?'

Trent stared at her for long, long seconds. 'Oh, sweet, dear Alethea, you've no idea, have you?'

'None at all,' she murmured. Sweet? Dear? What was happening? She felt dizzy trying to work it out. 'I—er—wouldn't mind if you—

um—told me a bit more,' she added huskily, her heart somersaulting away inside her body when Trent left the arm of his sofa and came over to the sofa where she was sitting.

With everything she had, she strove to appear normal as, sitting beside her, he turned to face her, studying her unsmiling expression for several moments before taking up her invitation to tell her more.

'You were going out that Friday—or so I believed,' he began. 'You, Alethea, not to put too fine a point on it, were getting between me and my every other thought.'

'Me?' she gasped.

'You,' he nodded. 'Which is why, since I acknowledged that for once in my life I clearly wasn't thinking straight, I saw a need for caution.'

'Yes,' she encouraged, none of this making sense so far. She put that down to the fact that Trent had the ability to scramble her brain like no one else she knew.

'I didn't think you were dating anyone seriously or, from what I thought I knew of you, you wouldn't have gone out with me the previous Tuesday.' He smiled. 'You were good enough to confirm it for me on Saturday. Anyhow, with you busy that Friday and me feeling a need for caution—yet at the same time needing like crazy to see you—I invented having a few people round the next night.'

'But—you hadn't invited anyone?'

'I could easily have done so, had you said yes. I had to think on my feet when I answered my door on Saturday—and there you were.'

'There probably wasn't any fog in Paris,' she commented weakly.

'There probably wasn't, but you were there—here in my home. I was ready to lie my head off if I had to. I'd been so certain you wouldn't come—I'd been planning to maybe stroll by your office on Monday.'

Alethea stared at him in amazement, having extreme difficulty taking in the fact that he had so wanted to see her he would have found a reason to call on her boss on the Monday when, casually, no doubt, he would have wandered into her office first. 'But—but you didn't have to—um—stroll by,' she recalled chokily. 'Not only did I come to your "party"—I also rang you Monday morning.'

'Oh, you did. Sweet love, you did.' He did nothing to decelerate her heart-rate. 'And I saw you twice that day. Once for me to hear what your difficulty was, and the second time for you to hear what I was going to do about it.'

'And did I hear about it!' she exclaimed, a shade sharply, she had to admit.

'You've every right to be angry,' Trent agreed. He startled her by taking her hands in a firm hold, as if fearful she might get up and rush away. 'But since I still feel that there was every need to do what I did, I can't ask you to forgive me.'

Alethea's emotions had been swinging first one way and then another. She felt hot, bothered and very much all over the place. And yet, at the same time, when her every instinct was to run, something was making her stay. Even though she was defeated by her knowledge that Trent's only reason for having her to live with him was from desire for her—which he had turned from when he'd had the opportunity—she had to stay.

'Still feel the need to do what you did?' she questioned, the fact that he had *not* taken her when he could have seeming to her to make a nonsense of that statement. 'This—er—desire business is—er—peculiar stuff!'

'Hell—it wasn't just desire!' he declared vehemently.

She stared at him dumbfounded. 'Wasn't it?' Confusion reigned supreme again.

Trent looked at her startled expression. 'Oh, love, have I been so successful in covering...? Have you no idea—?' Again he broke off. Then, his hands gripping hers, he seemed more resolute than ever. 'My dear Alethea,' he began determinedly, 'I wanted you to live with me, of course I did. And I desire you, of course I do. That is beyond doubt. But it's more than that.'

She was afraid to utter a word. It was more than desire? What was? 'Oh?' She mumbled a kind of question.

'I needed you to trust me,' he went on. 'Above all, I needed you to put your trust in me.'

'Trust?' She was no clearer.

'Perhaps I went the wrong way about it. Maybe I did. But I'd met your family, remember. And you'd already spoken—a couple of times—about finding somewhere else to live.' He paused, and then quietly revealed, 'It was important to me, Alethea, that we got to know each other better—without outside influences getting to you.'

It was important to him! Her heart started clamouring again. She swallowed hard, and knew that he had seen her nervousness, for he smiled, a gentle smile. 'Outside influences?' she picked out, and felt her backbone turn to water when Trent took one hand away from hers and stroked the backs of his fingers tenderly down one side of her face.

'By then I was aware of your upbringing, aware of the rancorous environment you'd grown up in.'

'My mother—' Alethea began defensively.

'She's your mother, and you love her,' he soothed. 'But I couldn't have her knocking down everything I was trying to achieve— which I was convinced, given half a chance, she would. You'd trusted me a little in that you'd dined with me, in that you'd come to my home, but that was light years away from the sort of trust, the commitment I needed.'

'You thought you'd get it by making me come and live with you?' Commitment?

'Poor love, I didn't give you much of a choice, did I?'

Her heart went wobbly again at his tenderly spoken 'poor love'. 'Trent,' she said helplessly, 'I just don't understand. Why did you want my trust. Why—?' She broke off. Both his hands were now holding her firmly by her upper arms.

'Why?' he answered, and left her staring in total disbelief when he quietly added, 'Because—I love you.'

She pulled back in shock. He held her firmly. 'You—love me!' she gasped.

'Had you no idea?' He seemed surprised.

She shook her head. 'None!' she answered. Trent *loved* her! Trent loved *her*!

'It—upsets you—worries you that I love you?' he asked, his voice, his look, tense and strained.

Dared she believe that he loved her? He'd already admitted,to telling one lie. She wasn't ready to answer. Far from being upset, or worried that her heart was going twenty to the dozen, she could not have been more ecstatic.

But to answer would only confirm what she was beginning to be sure he must know: that she was in love with him.

She tried to sound off-hand. She didn't do a very good job of it. 'You've lied to me once,' she reminded him.

'From necessity,' he owned straight away. 'From a need to cover this love I have for you, I've lied. But I'll never again lie to you. Trust me,' he urged.

Oh, she so wanted to, but she had to remind him, 'You lied to me a week after we met. When I came here and you said your friends were fog-bound in Paris, you lied. Are you saying...?'

'That it was necessary because I was in love with you then?' Trent moved his hands down to her hands; he gave them a little shake. 'That, my very dear love, *is* what I'm saying.'

He seemed sincere. 'Then?' she queried, unable to believe it.

'Then. Before then,' he stated, and went on making her eyes shoot wide again, 'I couldn't stop looking at you at Hector's Silver Wedding celebrations. When I came over to you, our eyes met—and that was it.'

'You l-loved me *then*!' She didn't believe it! How could she? Oh, Heavens, it would be all too wonderful if... But, it couldn't be...

'From the very beginning,' Trent assured her. 'Though if it's any help to you, I didn't believe it myself. I'd spoken to you—and you had a magical voice. I'd danced with you—and was overwhelmed to have you in my arms. So much so, I feared that like some callow youth I might there and then blurt out that I loved you. I had to get out of there. I felt an urgent need for caution.'

'That's why I didn't see you again that evening?' Somehow, what he was saying, even though she still dared not believe it, was starting to sound marginally credible.

'I knew your name and where you worked. I knew I'd see you again—to find out where you lived and your phone number was the easy part.'

'From what I've seen, and the way I contacted you over Keith Lawrence, I'd say everything fell into your lap.' Alethea started to cope with her shock. 'I even told you I intended moving out!'

'You're wonderful.' He smiled, but, his smile fading, he went on to reveal, 'A week after we met—that first Saturday you came here—I knew, had accepted, that my feelings were no figment of my imagination. I wanted you with me—I hadn't wanted to part from you when we'd dined together on Tuesday, and...'

'And you invited me back here for coffee,' she recalled.

'With no ulterior motive,' he assured her. 'While I was still cautious about this all-consuming emotion that had taken me, I just wanted to get to know you better. I was off to Italy in the morning, with no chance of seeing you again until Friday. I quite simply wanted to spend more time with you.'

Alethea wanted to tell him she was sorry that she hadn't done as he asked. But, while her wariness of what he had told her was diminishing, and belief was starting to burgeon, shyness seemed to be taking over.

'Instead you took me home.'

'Looking at you, I wanted like crazy to hold you in my arms again, to kiss you.'

'But you didn't.'

He smiled a half-smile. 'You'd got to me in a big way, Miss Pemberton—I was scared even to so much as shake you by the hand, in case the touch of your skin against mine sent my self-control flying.'

Alethea stared at him in amazement. He'd been feeling like that, and she'd never known! 'Heavens!' she mumbled.

'So there was I, ringing you as soon as I got in on Friday, only to know, for the first time in my life, that sick, stomach-churning emotion of jealousy. You were dating someone else.'

'I wasn't.' He'd been jealous! Trent had been jealous?

'I didn't know that then. All I knew was that I wanted to see you, and that if I had to invite your man-friend along then I'd do it. My God, talk about punishment!'

'I love you,' she said.

He froze. 'What did you say?' he commanded hoarsely.

'I d-don't believe I said it either!' she gasped. 'But...'

'But?' he demanded urgently.

She took a shaky breath. 'But, it's true,' she whispered shyly.

'You love me?' he insisted.

'I love you very much.'

'Come here.' Too impatient to wait, Trent caught hold of her in his arms, pulled her as close to him as he could. 'Never do I want to go through that again!' he breathed emphatically against her ear.

'I'm sorry,' she murmured.

'Say it again.'

'I'm sorry.'

'Not that.'

She laughed, a light, relieved, wonderful laugh. 'I love you,' she obeyed, and as he pulled back from her to look into her face, into her eyes, to see the truth there for himself, she added shyly, 'to distraction.'

'Oh, my love!' He exhaled a shaky pent-up breath and kissed her. Alethea's eyes were shining when Trent pulled back. He studied her, and he just had to embrace her again. 'When did you know?' he asked, after breaking his kiss but keeping her in his arms.

She was happy to be there. 'That I loved you?'

'How marvellous that sounds,' he breathed. 'When?' he pressed.

'It had been coming on for a long while.' She hesitated no longer in telling him. 'I knew I was affected by you that first time we met.'

'Good. And?'

'Well, I suppose there have been few times when we've been together when you haven't managed to make me thoroughly confused.'

'You confessed that to me once—I found it most heartening,' he revealed, laying a tender kiss against her cheek.

Her heart fluttered, but the way it had been cavorting this past hour she doubted it would ever be the same again. 'Then there was the jealousy...'

'My jealousy?'

'Mine,' she said.

He frowned. 'But I've never given you cause to be jealous. I haven't been remotely interested in any other woman since I met you. How could I be? I eat, drink and sleep you. You're everywhere in my head, night and day. Sometimes I've thought I'd go demented just—'

'You say the most wonderful things,' Alethea interrupted him with a sigh.

Trent placed another tender kiss on the corner of her mouth. 'So tell me, before I get totally sidetracked,' he insisted, placing yet one more kiss on the other corner of her mouth, 'what it was I did to cause you to feel jealous.'

Her skin was tingling from his tender kisses. Sitting here with him like this, knowing that he loved her, feeling secure in that love, she knew she would deny him nothing. She knew that there was much unsaid, but with no secrets between them now, they should share everything with each other.

'You didn't have to do very much for that dreadful green-eyed monster to take a grip on my imagination,' she admitted. 'In fact, you didn't have to do anything.' Trent sat quietly looking at her—she knew he was waiting for her to go on. 'Well, the first time—and I didn't know how I felt about you then—'

'You loved me,' Trent interrupted, surprising her that he seemed to need to hear her say again that she loved him.

'I loved you,' she obliged with a tender smile, and was allowed to go on. 'That day, the day I—we'd arranged for me to—er—move in with you...'

'It was a Wednesday.' He had instant recall.

'Well, I'd very mixed feelings about what I was doing.'

'How you must have hated me.'

'I tried,' she laughed. 'Anyhow, that was the day Nick Saunders asked me out and—' She broke off. Trent wasn't smiling. 'Don't be upset—you've nothing to be...'

'Jealous over?'

'It's you I love.'

Trent took a controlling breath. 'I can't think why you should—only—never stop.'

She kissed him; he seemed to like it, and she had an uphill job to remember what she had been telling him. It was incredible just to be in his arms. 'Anyhow, it was only then that it dawned on me that I was no longer free to go out with someone else if I wanted to.'

'You turned him down?'

'Of course, but then started to wonder if you were thinking the same way.'

'If I'd given up dating other women while you were living with me?'

Alethea nodded. 'While I didn't recognise my jealousy then, I most definitely didn't care for the notion of you seeing other women.'

'You were jealous,' Trent decided, and seemed quite pleased.

'Wretch!' she called him lovingly. 'Nor was that the end of it.'

'Tell me more,' he urged—and she just had to laugh.

'There was I, reluctant to move in, in panic and delaying the evil moment. But, after delaying no longer, I arrived, and there are you about to go out!'

'Hmm. Want to hear about another lie?' he asked.

'Another one?'

'Originally I'd no intention of going out that evening. I'd come home early and very nearly wore a track in the carpet walking up and down waiting for you.'

'Really!' she exclaimed.

'Believe it. I'll never lie to you again,' he reiterated. 'I'd planned a pleasant evening getting to know each other in a friendly way, building up your trust in me if I could. Whether you knew it or not you'd already started to trust me a little when the day before you'd phoned and asked, just that one small but magical heart-pounding word "when" in relation to moving in. I wanted so much from that first evening when you did move in. I wanted you to learn to like me—only—where *were* you?'

'I'd no idea you wanted...'

'Of course you hadn't, sweet love. So there was I, getting disgruntled. So that, by the time you did turn up, I found I was excusing my initial grumpiness by telling you I had to go out. Following on from that, if I didn't want you to take me for a liar, I had to do just that.'

'Heavens!' she gasped, and she thought she'd suffered! Alethea was still a little open-mouthed when she owned, 'I was both peeved and jealous that, on my first evening, you were probably going out with some woman.'

'You're adorable,' he murmured, and her backbone wilted.

'Oh, Trent,' she said shakily.

'Are you having a hard time believing it too?' he asked.

'It does seem fairly incredible,' she admitted, and they kissed, and it *was* incredible—to be in his arms, with all the barriers falling.

'When I returned that night, I came to your room,' Trent confessed.

'I know,' she replied dreamily.

'You knew! I woke you? Oh, God—did I panic you?'

'I think I was a bit worried, but...'

'Oh, I'm so sorry. I thought I was being quiet. I just couldn't believe you were here under my roof. I just had to check.'

'I was already awake. But I slept like a log afterwards,' she smiled. 'And I heard you go out the next morning,' she added impishly.

Trent grinned. 'I came back. I had to. Love was ruling me. I'd only just gone when I realised I couldn't wait until evening to see you again. I thought that perhaps you'd need an alarm call!'

'I was already up.'

'And in your blue robe, looking positively adorable. Is it any wonder, so soon after you began living with me, I had to break all my good intentions and kiss you.'

'Oh, that you did,' she smiled.

'And the bonus was, you took it at face value. Could *I* take it that you trusted me a little bit more?'

'I remember being confused, but I wasn't scared,' she admitted.

'I was,' he confessed. 'I reached my office realising that while I was going to protect you, who was going to protect me? I realised that I was in a more vulnerable position than I felt you were. All that day, my longing to see you grew and grew, so that, by the end of it, I'd reached such a pitch I feared I might give away how desperately I cared for you. It was I, my love, who delayed going home that night.'

'You weren't working late?' she queried, wide-eyed.

'I made myself work late. But there was no need, nor the next night either.'

Slowly it was coming home to Alethea just how very deeply Trent did love her. All her feelings went out to him, and it seemed to her then that he must know she cared as much about him. 'I do love you, oh, so much,' she told him.

'Keep telling me,' he urged, and they clung together and kissed tenderly, as though sealing their love.

They stayed close against each other as uncounted minutes ticked by. Trent saluted her face, her eyes, with tiny kisses, touching her arms, her shoulders, her face and her hair as if he rejoiced to have her there, yet at the same time still feared she might disappear.

Yet it was Alethea, as they drew back to look in each other's eyes, who asked, 'Am I dreaming?'

'It's not a dream,' Trent murmured adoringly. 'It's a wonderful, heartfelt reality.' She kissed him and smiled as he returned the compliment, before he tucked her neatly into his shoulder where she made a perfect fit. 'Although I thought I was dreaming that wonderful Saturday morning when you brought me a cup of tea in bed. You *must* have been starting to trust me.'

'Oh, I must,' she smiled. After having endured so much tearing of her emotions, now at last, she was starting to feel her heart ease, a state that came from knowing, and be-lieving, oneself to be loved in return. 'I was beginning to love you then, I think.'

'You were?' He moved her so he could see into her face again. Giving her a little shake, he pressed, 'You're not going to leave it there, are you?'

She laughed. Oh, Heavens, how much she loved him! 'I remember I didn't feel all that happy when you said you were going to be out of the country for three weeks,' she re-plied demurely, and received a tender squeeze for that admission.

'We spent the day together,' he instantly re-called. 'And what a day it was.'

'You—er—enjoyed it?'

'When I wasn't furious with you that you'd found yourself somewhere else to live! Not only did you have the nerve to tell me about it, but you had the gall to tell me that I knew our living together was not a permanent ar-rangement—when I knew nothing of the sort!'

Alethea's heart took yet another leap. Was Trent saying he would like her to live with him permanently? Even while she was starting to become more and more secure in the love he had for her, she did not like to ask.

'I—er—didn't think you'd mind.'

'Mind? I was incensed! Though—' he smiled '—I tried to be rational. I almost offered to get the decorators in for you, I remember.'

'Did you?' she asked, surprised.

'I said, almost,' he grinned. 'That was the instinctive part, the part that wanted to make things easy for you. That was before I quickly realised that, dammit, I didn't want you to have a flat ready to move into. I didn't want you to leave.'

'I wasn't too much of a nuisance, then?' she teased, 'Living in your house, I mean.'

'Nuisance?' he echoed. 'Bothersome, I'd say. It was like treading on eggs the whole time you were around.'

Alethea was amazed. 'How?' she exclaimed.

'My stars, do you have a lot to learn about the male of the species,' Trent murmured. 'Which, of course, I shall be only too pleased to teach you. But, for the moment, leave it that, having got you in my home and living under my roof, the patience I was trying to exercise almost straight away began to be irksome.'

'Patience?'

'Never my best quality,' he smiled. 'I hardly ever seemed to see you, and when I did—while all the time I was endeavouring to gain more and more of your trust—it was such a joy to have you here that I seemed to be spending most of my time fighting the compulsion to touch your hand in passing, to drop a light kiss in your hair.'

'Oh, Trent,' she sighed blissfully, her confidence in his love for her growing with every wonderful word he spoke. 'You kissed me, that Saturday when we spent the day together.'

'On the bridge over the brook.' He needed no reminding. 'And you kissed me back, and I had to consider, had I gone about everything in the wrong way?'

'I'm not with you.'

'We were away from the house. Away from anything threatening, when you returned my kisses. Was that why you seemed so relaxed? I couldn't decide. All I knew was that if I was to earn the complete trust I needed from you,

I was going to have to take the greatest care. Yet when we arrived back that night, my darling, I discovered, when I again kissed you, when it was I who wanted your trust—that I didn't trust myself! Only by the skin of my teeth did I manage to turn away from you.'

Good Heavens! She remembered feeling a bit miffed about that. As Trent had said, it seemed she had a lot to learn. 'Er—you kissed me again the next morning,' she reminded him, though in view of the ardent way she had responded, somewhat shyly.

'I couldn't go away without seeing you again, so I used bringing you a cup of tea as an excuse. I kissed you and you asked me to stop. The demands you've made on my self-control, woman,' he growled.

'I didn't want you to—er—stop, not really,' she felt she should let him know.

'My G—' He didn't finish. 'Come here,' he threatened, and kissed her breathless for her trouble.

Alethea was pink-cheeked when Trent finally allowed a little daylight between their two bodies. 'I—er—you phoned, while you were away,' she mentioned, in an effort to try and get her head back to somewhere near normal. 'You rang that first Monday you were away.'

'I just had to give in to the need to hear your voice,' Trent revealed.

'Oh,' she sighed. 'I left work on time on Tuesday, but you didn't phone.'

'Oh, sweetheart.'

'It's all right,' she said swiftly, when Trent seemed full of remorse. 'You rang Wednesday.'

'Several times, before you finally answered.'

'Was that why you bit my head off?' she teased, remembering their sharp exchange over the phone.

'I was upset—and,' he admitted, 'as jealous as the devil. Where were you? Who with? You didn't make me any sweeter when, to my mind, your home was with me and you made no bones about telling me you'd been decorating your flat. The way I saw it then, if I didn't hurry up and finish my business in South America, you'd have moved out before I got home.'

'Oh, darling,' she said softly, 'I didn't mean to upset you.'

'Upset me!' She rather guessed that was an understatement. 'I was going quietly insane. Every time I phoned after that, you were never in. I...'

'You rang again?'

'Frequently. Evenings, Saturday afternoon, Sunday afternoon.'

'I must have been decorating—or at my mother's.'

'Thank God I didn't know who you were decorating with!'

'I'm too much in love with you to be interested in anyone else,' she stated quietly, and was soundly kissed.

'Oh, sweet darling,' he breathed.

Alethea snuggled up to him. 'So you decided to come home early?'

'I was so stewed up because you were never there to answer my phone calls, and I resolved to get my work done with all speed. Matters were very definitely not working out the way I'd planned.'

'How had you planned matters?' she asked prettily.

'Baggage!' he becalled her lovingly. Then willingly explained, 'As I've said, I'd met your mother and saw at once that she was a deeply embittered woman. I met your sister too— she seemed to be heading the same way.'

'She was probably apprehensive and a little mixed up,' Alethea explained. 'She knew— when you didn't—that her husband had robbed you and that he'd been suspended.'

'It's a funny old world,' Trent smiled. 'There was I, needing some way to assist you in following through your intention of leaving your family home. And there you were, that Monday lunchtime, almost in the same breath as you informed me of your brother-in-law's misdemeanours daring to tell me you'd made up your mind not to see me again.' He broke off to tap her nose with his forefinger. 'Sweet love, I wasn't having that.'

'So you devised your devious plan,' she teased.

'It didn't take much planning. In fact, it was so simple, it was as though Fate had dropped the answer in my lap. There was no way I would have prosecuted Lawrence anyhow.'

'You wouldn't?' she gasped.

'I was in love with you. If I hurt your sister it would hurt you.'

'Just a minute—you're saying you wouldn't have prosecuted Keith Lawrence whether I came to live here or whether I didn't?'

Her answer was in his grin. 'Hate me?' he queried.

'To distraction,' she purred, and kissed him. But then she remembered something, and moved a little away from him.

'What is it?' he asked urgently, his eyes not missing the brief shadow that had crossed her face.

'Why didn't you...? I mean—Tuesday. Tuesday morning, when you came home from South America. Why...?' She was starting to feel a shade warm around the cheeks, but fortunately Trent understood, and she didn't have to go any further.

First of all, he gently kissed her brow. 'My darling, never think I didn't want you. You'll never know—' He broke off. 'I should explain,' he said, and went on, 'I'd worked like blazes to get back to you all the sooner and, having arrived home five days ahead of schedule, I just had to quietly open your bedroom door. Forgive me, I couldn't resist a glimpse of you.'

'Only I wasn't there,' she put in gently.

'I'd never felt so let down in my life. I was feeling sick inside as I went along to my own room. I opened my door, went over and switched on a bedside light—and couldn't believe my eyes.'

'I—er—was lonesome for you,' she confessed.

'Were you, love?' She could tell he wanted to hear more.

'I'd been unsettled for some while,' she obliged. 'Then on Saturday I was so restless I rang Nick Saunders and took him out to dinner—a kind of thank-you for all the work he'd put in on the decorating.'

'Did you, now?'

His tone was quiet, but she wouldn't have liked it, either, had he confessed to taking some woman out. 'I stayed the night at my flat—alone, of course,' she told him hurriedly. 'The next morning, I knew what had been staring me in the face for some while: that I was in love with you.'

'You knew on Sunday?'

She nodded. 'If it makes you feel any better, I've had a miserable time of it,' she owned.

'I've never wanted you to be hurt,' he murmured.

'Hurt, unable to eat, sleepless. I couldn't sleep on Monday night,' she confessed. 'I— er—wanted to feel close to you. The closest I could think of, when insomnia took a hold, was to go and get into your bed. But...'

'But you never expected me to arrive back early,' Trent filled in for her. 'And I, having put that lamp on, having seen you there, was afraid to put it out again in case I disturbed you. I got into bed with no intent, believe me, other than, after not having seen you for over two weeks, to let the salve of being that close to you wash over me.'

'But I woke up.'

'I was determined to keep everything light so you shouldn't be alarmed, but I nearly tripped up when I told you I'd been looking forward to seeing you—it so nearly came out *longing* to see you. All the while I was wondering what, if anything, I could assume from the fact you'd chosen to sleep in my bed.'

'Oh, dear,' she commented. 'I was afraid you'd be much too clever.'

'Clever!' he discounted. 'Even while I was fairly certain you wouldn't have elected to sleep in my bed if you hated me, I've been in hell—unable to decide if that then meant that you cared for me in any degree . . . and how I should set about finding out.'

'We kissed,' she offered.

'And that got out of hand too.'

'Was that why you stopped—er—kissing?' she asked, more and more confident that he did love her as he'd declared, but still mightily unsure of why things had ended up the way they had that night.

Trent cradled her close and placed an adoring kiss in her hair. 'Sweetest Alethea, matters had gone so far between us by then that, but for a brief moment when shyness caused a hiccup in your wonderful response, I would have made you mine.'

'It—er—was my fault?'

He laughed. 'What a darling you are. No, my innocent, it was mine. If fault there be, it was all mine. In that moment when you backed away, I had a split second in which to

wonder what I thought I was doing. Was this
the way to gain your trust? By taking
advantage . . .'

'I did trust you,' she said softly.

'Sweet love,' he breathed. 'That's what I
counter-argued with myself. Surely you must
have trusted me, or what were you doing in
my bed? But, remember, all the time I was
wanting you like crazy. You hadn't known
that I'd be sharing that bed when you'd decided to sleep there. I was losing it fast,
Alethea,' he confided. 'My brain was alive
with argument; while all the while I was trying
to deny my desire for you, I was also trying
to decide what was best for you.'

Alethea was little short of amazed that
Trent had been having such a tremendous
battle within himself. 'You decided that I'd
better go back to my own bed?'

'I couldn't hope to think clearly while you
were still there with me. I needed you to know
that I would never let you down—yet wasn't
I letting you down by seducing you?'

'From where I was viewing it, the—um—
seduction was—er—pretty mutual,' she offered shyly.

'Oh, sweetheart. You were so vulnerable then, and I knew it. I needed to think, but you were still there. My homecoming dream was turning into a nightmare!'

'So, I'd already intimated that I'd go if you put out the light, and you switched it off!'

'And spent the next few hours after you'd gone trying, with little success, to get my head back together.'

'You didn't sleep?'

'Did you?' She shook her head, and he smiled. 'Early-morning tea in bed came in useful again when I resolved we'd reached the end of the road; we had to talk.'

'You brought me tea, and I was terrified you'd seen that I loved you.'

'And I was terrified, hoping that you did. I came home early that night, but you didn't.'

'I was running scared, as you discovered when you ran me to earth at the flat.'

He grinned, but was serious again when he owned, 'I was ready to commit murder when that man walked in familiarly, wanting to celebrate his efforts in your bedroom.'

'Perhaps he could have phrased it better,' she allowed.

Trent took a moment out to kiss her, but then said, 'So much for my daring to believe you might care for me a little. All too obviously while I'd been out of the country, you'd been doing very nicely, thank you. It was more than flesh and blood could stand.'

'I don't suppose I helped very much with my ''cheap'' remark. I didn't know then that you loved me,' she added.

'So I was hurting like hell,' he growled. 'Who said love made you rational?'

'You're not hurting now?' she asked urgently.

'Now, I've never felt better.'

She relaxed again. 'You didn't send my belongings over—you said you would.'

'That was before I'd cooled down sufficiently to begin analysing events. That was when this notion I'd had, that you might care a little, came back and wouldn't go away. But, in the state I was in, it seemed to me that, after the way we'd parted, you had to make the first move. Everything had started with my belief that you should learn to trust me.'

'You still wanted my trust?'

'You had to trust me—trust me enough to come to me. To my way of thinking—though your pride could have prevented it—you had a good excuse because your clothes were still here.'

'Clever,' she murmured softly. 'That was exactly the excuse I did use, of course.'

Trent kissed the tip of her nose, but was solemn-eyed when he revealed, 'The waiting was interminable. Thoughts of you filled most every waking moment. I couldn't sleep, I couldn't eat—and where were you? You didn't call, you didn't phone.'

'Oh, Trent,' she whispered. She'd had no idea it had been like that for him.

He smiled then as he confessed, 'My dear, I've spent this day slowly reaching breaking point. I had, in fact, just decided I must re-think everything. The only certainty in my head and heart was that I must have you in my life—then, the doorbell rang.'

How absolutely fantastic it was to hear those words 'I must have you in my life'! Alethea swallowed emotionally. 'And—there I was,' she managed huskily.

'And there you were,' he breathed. 'I couldn't believe it. There was a roaring in my ears, a thundering in my heart which—until I'd got myself under some kind of control—I had to fight, with all I had, to hide.'

'Oh, darling,' she sighed, and gently kissed him, and was gently kissed in return. 'Now there's no need for either of us to hide how we feel.'

'No more, never again,' Trent murmured tenderly. But then he caused her to still, as he went on, 'Alethea, my dear, my life; I wanted you to come and live with me because I wanted you to learn to trust me, to get used to me, to hopefully see that making some kind of commitment is not so awful as I'm certain you've been brought up to believe. But, sweet love, I want, need, more than that.'

Alethea stared at him. She wasn't sure what he was saying. But, since they were never going to hide anything ever again, she confessed, 'I thought I wanted a place of my own, but I don't.'

'Because?' he pressed.

'Because...' She took a deep breath. 'Because I only want to live with you,' she whispered.

'Oh, love,' Trent breathed, brushing the backs of his fingers against her hair. One arm was firmly around her when, his expression serious, sincere, he asked, 'Enough—to marry me?'

'Marry...!' she gasped, and Trent held her steady.

'I've known, from that first time we went out together, you find the idea of marriage appalling,' he stated quickly. 'But ever since that Saturday, a week after I met you, when you asked me had I quite finished, and I told you I hadn't yet started, I've known that I intend to marry you.'

'You—have?' she managed huskily.

'Say you will,' he urged. 'I know you've a hang-up about it, but together we can—'

'I—er—don't have—er—any particular—hang-up.' Alethea found her voice to interrupt, when she had her breath back; Trent had actually asked her to marry him!

'You—don't?'

'Had I still been living at home, I might...'
She stopped. 'Perhaps that's unfair.' She
smiled. 'You, Mr de Havilland, have
somehow turned my world upside-down.
That, plus my love and trust in you, have
made a nonsense of any preconceived ideas I
might have had in relation to marriage and—
er—my non-participation in such...'

Trent couldn't wait for her to finish. 'Does
that mean yes?' he demanded. 'You love me,
you trust me... You'll—marry me?'

'I'd like very much to marry you,' she accepted, and didn't know if the noise in her
ears came from herself or Trent, as he let out
a joyous sound and hugged her and covered
her face with kisses.

'Oh, Alethea,' he breathed. 'Alethea, I can
hardly believe that you've just agreed to
marry me. I've been in such hell,' he groaned
against her throat.

'Oh, darling,' she whispered, her face
against his face. 'I don't want you to hurt any
more.'

'Little love,' he breathed, pulling back to
look adoringly into her face. 'I've hurt you

too. Without meaning to, I've hurt you. Forgive me.'

Alethea leaned forward and kissed him. There was nothing to forgive. He loved her.

MILLS & BOON® PUBLISH EIGHT
LARGE PRINT TITLES A MONTH.
THESE ARE THE EIGHT TITLES
FOR OCTOBER 1997

———————— ❧ ————————

ACCIDENTAL NANNY
Lindsay Armstrong

HUSBAND BY CONTRACT
Helen Brooks

THE MARRIAGE WAR
Charlotte Lamb

TWO-WEEK WIFE
Miranda Lee

LONG NIGHT'S LOVING
Anne Mather

SOLUTION: SEDUCTION!
Elizabeth Oldfield

THE TROUBLE WITH TRENT!
Jessica Steele

A MARRIAGE HAS BEEN ARRANGED
Anne Weale

MILLS & BOON® PUBLISH EIGHT
LARGE PRINT TITLES A MONTH.
THESE ARE THE EIGHT TITLES
FOR NOVEMBER 1997

———————— ❦ ————————

SEDUCING THE ENEMY
Emma Darcy

THE NINETY-DAY WIFE
Emma Goldrick

SETTLING THE SCORE
Sharon Kendrick

TWO-PARENT FAMILY
Patricia Knoll

WILDEST DREAMS
Carole Mortimer

A TYPICAL MALE!
Sally Wentworth

ACCIDENTAL MISTRESS
Cathy Williams

COURTING TROUBLE
Patricia Wilson